THE GOOD NAZI

THE GOOD NAZI

SAMIR MACHADO DE MACHADO

TRANSLATED FROM THE PORTUGUESE
BY RAHUL BERY

Pushkin Press
Somerset House, Strand
London WC2R 1LA

O Crime do Bom Nazista
© Samir Machado de Machado, 2023
Published in agreement with Redondo Books International Literary Agency
English translation © Rahul Bery, 2025

First published by Pushkin Press in 2025

Obra publicada com o apoio da Fundação Biblioteca Nacional, do Ministério da Cultura do Brasil, e do Instituto Guimarães Rosa, do Ministério das Relações Exteriores do Brasil / Work published with the support of the National Library Foundation of the Brazilian Ministry of Culture and the Guimarães Rosa Institute of the Brazilian Ministry of Foreign Affairs

ISBN 13: 978-1-80533-533-7

All rights reserved. No part of this publication may be reproduced, stored in a retrieval system or transmitted in any form or by any means, electronic, mechanical, photocopying, recording or otherwise, without prior permission in writing from Pushkin Press

The authorised representative in the EEA is
eucomply OÜ, Pärnu mnt. 139b-14, 11317, Tallinn, Estonia,
hello@eucompliancepartner.com, +33757690241

Designed and typeset by Tetragon, London
Printed and bound in the United Kingdom by Clays Ltd, Elcograf S.p.A.

Pushkin Press is committed to a sustainable future for our business, our readers and our planet. This book is made from paper from forests that support responsible forestry.

www.pushkinpress.com

1 3 5 7 9 8 6 4 2

Forget about what you are escaping from.
Reserve your anxiety for what you are escaping to.

MICHAEL CHABON
The Amazing Adventures of Kavalier & Clay

gondola

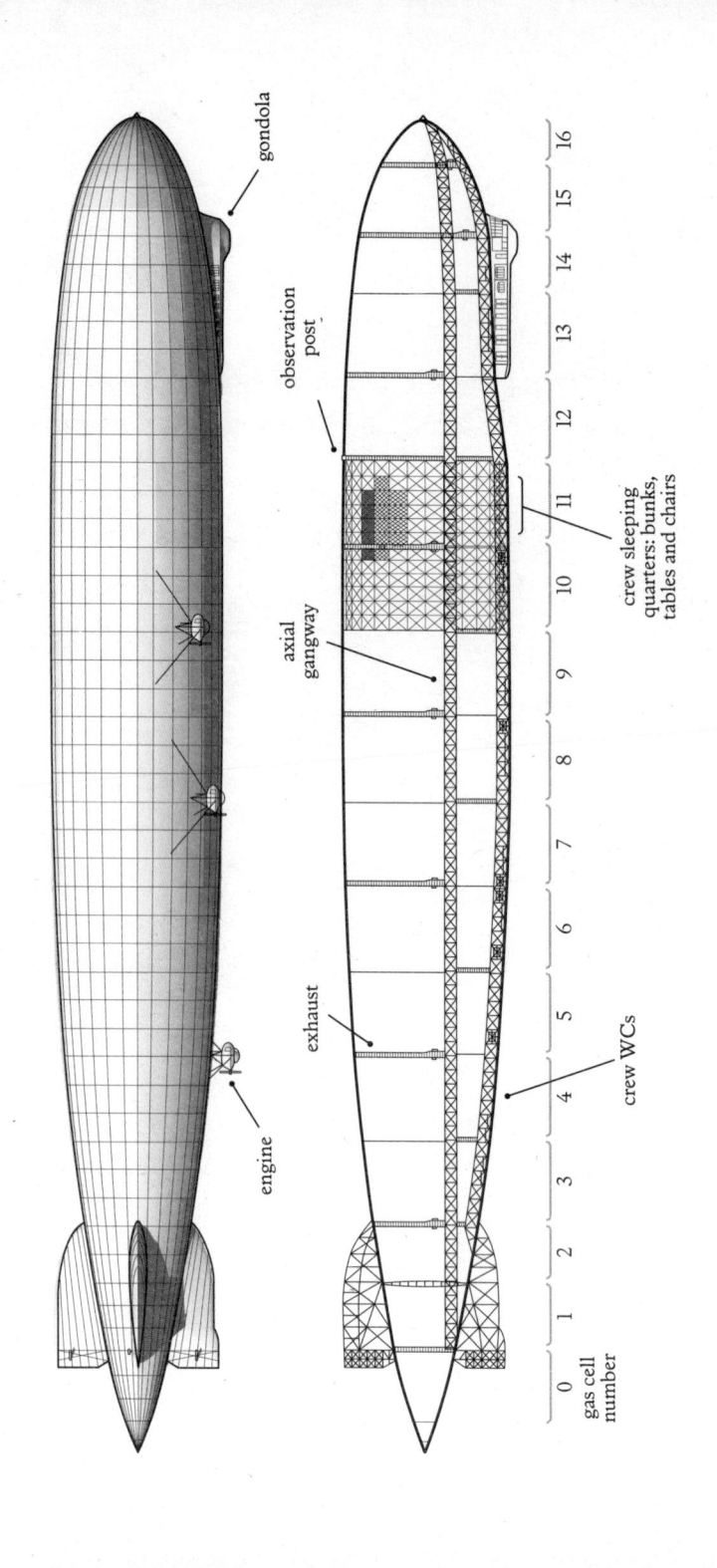

observation post

axial gangway

exhaust

engine

crew sleeping quarters: bunks, tables and chairs

crew WCs

gas cell number 0 1 2 3 4 5 6 7 8 9 10 11 12 13 14 15 16

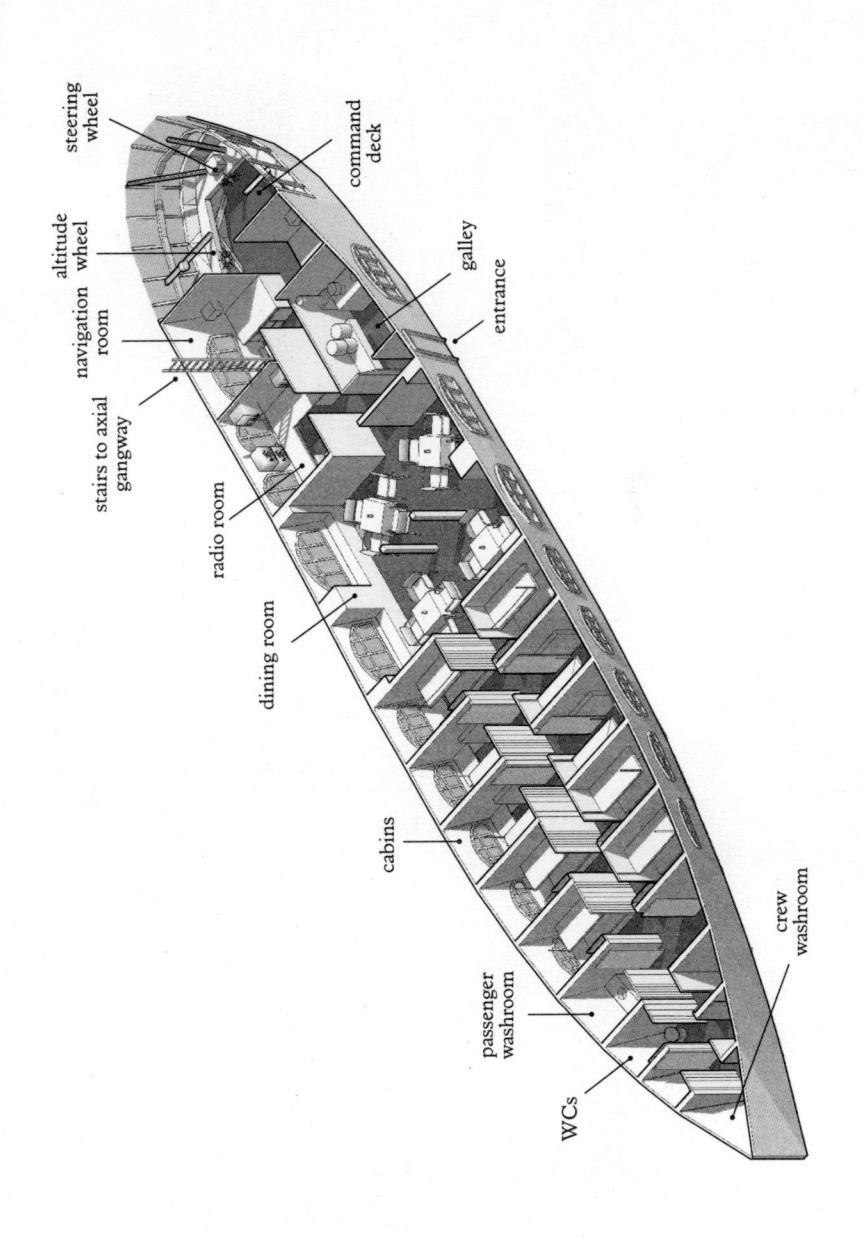

Diagram of the LZ 127 *Graf Zeppelin* and its gondola

One

It emerged like a Valkyrie in the skies of Recife, advancing through the clouds with a serenity that concealed its rapid progress. Viewed head-on, it was just a silver disc, a shimmering shield. However, as it moved it was moulded by the light which struck its every surface, its graceful shape disguising the astonishing reality: at that very moment, sixty-seven tonnes were floating elegantly over the state of Pernambuco.

Three years earlier, its first passage through the city had been the occasion for a municipal holiday and had brought huge crowds onto the streets. But this was not the first of its many trips to Brazil, nor would it be the last. There were ten per year in total between the months of June and October, undertaken with German regularity, and there had never been any accidents. Although there were no longer any holidays or crowds, the airship still drew fascinated gazes, from people staring out of their windows, children on the street and anyone else whose routine was interrupted by the sight of that 230-metre colossus.

It was four in the afternoon when the ropes were tied to the mooring mast and the LZ 127 *Graf Zeppelin* landed in Campo do Jiquiá, Recife. The first to board were the customs officers, the maritime police and the port health authorities, to carry out their inspection. Then the passengers disembarked. For some, it was their final destination. For others, taken by car to the Hotel Central, it was the last opportunity, after nearly three days spent crossing the Atlantic, to stretch their legs or smoke (which, naturally, was not permitted on board), before continuing their journey for a further day and a half to Rio de Janeiro.

Hotel Central was the tallest building in town, a yellow tower built in the style that had only recently come to be called art deco. Its seventh-floor restaurant provided a panoramic view over the city. A group of tables was reserved for the passengers of the Luftschiffbau Zeppelin, both those in transit and those still waiting to board.

Among them, seated alone at a table, was a man in a dark suit.

The passport in his breast pocket would have revealed the following details: Name: Bruno Brückner. Age:

thirty-two. Build: medium. Face shape: oval. Eye colour: grey. Place of birth: Berlin. Occupation: *Kriminalpolizei*, police detective. A recent scar on the right side of his face, running from the temple to the middle of his cheek, lent a certain air of danger to his features, which, otherwise, gave off a neutral, distant look of indifference. The swastika pin attached to his suit showed affiliation to the party which was gradually permeating every aspect of German daily life.

Bruno was drinking his whisky and soda, reading a recent edition of *Aurora Alemã* (German Dawn), the Nazi party's weekly magazine, published by the embassy in São Paulo. The news, several months out of date, reported how, after having gained a majority in the Reichstag and thus consecrating their leader as chancellor, the Nazis were now passing the Enabling Act, which gave absolute power to the Führer to create laws without being inconvenienced by parliament or the courts.

Bruno put the newspaper to one side. He took a brown paper envelope from his waistcoat pocket and, from inside it, removed a card his nephew had given him at the train station in Berlin before he departed for the LZ airfield in Friedrichshafen. In the child's drawing, the airship was smiling like a big flying whale. Little Josef had drawn his uncle inside that whale, wearing a hat and with his hand raised in farewell, as if he were the proverbial biblical prophet.

Bruno smiled, put the card back into the envelope, returned it to his pocket and picked up the newspaper again. The news was always delivered in the same tedious and optimistic tone of the party propaganda that was now the voice of a government which sought to fuse the party into the national identity: being German would necessarily come to mean being a Nazi. Faithful to its beliefs in German racial superiority, the newspaper adhered to its totalitarian motto: *"Deutschland über alles. Germany above all… love it or leave it."*

Bruno grew tired of the newspaper and looked around the dining room, seeking to identify which of his travel companions from the days spent over the ocean would stay on as part of the group continuing to Rio. His discreet habits meant he had not interacted with them much. During the journey, he had chosen to rise early and have breakfast alone, before everyone else, and had spent most of his time reading, either in the dining room or in his cabin, which prevented others from striking up conversation with him. His gruff air was also justified by the lack of any sights to admire during the past few days: no matter which window you looked out of, all you could see was the tedious and endless Atlantic horizon. He had sought not to arouse the interest of any of the other passengers, who barely noticed him, or, if they did, took him for a shy recluse.

There were some new faces among those present, but one seemed familiar. This man was of a similar age to him, with jet black hair that was combed back and set rigidly in place with gleaming Brilliantine. He was also sitting alone and, despite the heat, wore a black overcoat, as if he expected an improbable winter to arrive in the city at any moment. He was cradling a leather briefcase in his hands, protectively, and for an instant Bruno felt the other man was staring at him. He stared back at him and the man, out of instinct or politeness, looked away and went back to letting his gaze wander around the dining room, sombre and blasé as if in a Tamara de Lempicka painting.

Bruno did not remember having seen the man on board and thus assumed he was a guest at the hotel or a passenger waiting to be taken to the boarding gate. He finished his whisky and soda just seconds before a member of the hotel staff came to announce that the taxis that would take them back to the Zeppelin were waiting for them at the entrance. When he got up, he noticed the man with the briefcase had also risen and was heading to the lift with the others.

So, he was a passenger, Bruno concluded.

At half past six the sun went down and the taxis returned the passengers to Campo do Jiquiá. As they entered the Zeppelin, just as when they had boarded in

Germany, each passenger was given a white linen napkin inside a personalized envelope, which each one of them had to keep and reuse until the end of the journey, apparently to reduce the weight on board. Bruno could not see what difference half a dozen napkins would make to the tonnage of that Leviathan and suspected that this was done to compensate for the lack of laundry facilities.

As soon as he entered his cabin, Bruno saw that another whisky and soda was waiting for him on the table by the window. It was one of those little details which had garnered such high praise for the service. Next to the drink was a typed list with the names of all the passengers on board. He noticed a greater number of Brazilian names, passengers with surnames like Botelho, Tavares, Correia, almost always men and almost all with the same occupation: commerce.

It was understandable. Just to go on that journey of a day and a half between Recife and Rio, sailing through the air, feeling like a character in a Jules Verne novel, would cost you 1,400 reichsmarks. The trip was a small extravagance these men had permitted themselves and, in some cases, their wives.

Likewise, Bruno had indulged himself. He could have come to Brazil by ship, it would certainly have been cheaper, but he did not like the idea of spending two weeks bobbing up and down on the high seas. And as there were no transatlantic passenger aircraft, the only other possible way for a passenger to cross the Atlantic from Europe to South America was to travel through the air on the Luftschiffbau Zeppelin.

When he looked at the list, he also noticed that a single new German name had appeared since their departure from Friedrichshafen: Otto Klein. This, he concluded, was the name of the fellow from the hotel.

Bruno sat down on the sofa, drank his whisky and soda and contemplated the turf on the airfield. The truth was, there wasn't much to do on board except eat, sleep and socialize—the passenger gondola was not much bigger than a luxury train wagon. In the prow were situated the command deck, the navigation room, the radio room and the tiny galley for food preparation—which boasted of being the world's first to be made of aluminium. And on either side of a narrow corridor running through the stern was a row of small but comfortable cabins. At the end of the corridor were the WCs and washrooms.

At eight o'clock in the evening, once the postbags had been delivered and collected and the sixteen enormous gasbags had been refilled with hydrogen, the ropes were cut and the Zeppelin departed. Soon after it had taken flight, the chief steward knocked on the door of each cabin, informing the passengers that dinner would be served shortly.

Bruno pulled his suitcase over and unpacked his things before leaving the cabin, whose sofa would be dismantled by the room attendant and made up as a bed. He made his way to the dining room which dominated the centre of the Zeppelin's gondola. After examining each one of the passengers in turn, Bruno sat at an empty table—the one nearest to the prow, next to the starboard windows.

The wooden chairs were upholstered with elegant floral prints, the tables draped with fine linen tablecloths, the wallpaper decorated with art nouveau arabesques and the windows framed by curtains. The place gave off a pleasantly nostalgic feeling as if, while on board, one could return to the world as it was before the Great War.

But a return to that world of abundant luxuries and comforts would also inevitably mean a return to imminent war, for that had been the natural consequence of those times. He had been twelve when the war began and sixteen when it ended. That had been his adolescence. And who in the world, thought Bruno, having reached adulthood, would really want to relive such an adolescence?

Two

FAITHFUL to the nationalist spirit of the time, the gastronomic experience offered by Zeppelin on board its airships was not the best of *global* cuisine, but rather the best of *German* cuisine, which, we can safely say, no one ever accused of being light and refined, but to which all due respect must be given for having provoked in its people a persistent questioning of the meaning of existence, aiding the formation of many generations of great philosophers. Over the course of the journey, however, some concessions had to be made to local cuisines as they restocked at each stop, guaranteeing some variety at the dining table.

Bruno picked up from the table that evening's menu typed out in German and Portuguese and printed on card with the LZ letterhead:

Auf See zwischen Pernambuco/
Rio de Janeiro 16/10/1933
At sea between Pernambuco and
Rio de Janeiro 16/10/1933

Reisen no 257	Voyage no 257
Abendessen	*Dinner*
Tapiokasuppe	Tapioca soup
Kalbfleisch in Sahnesauce mit Spaghetti	Veal in cream sauce with spaghetti
Geröstete Pfifferlinge	Roasted chanterelles
Salat aux fines herbes	Salade aux fines herbes
Verschiedene Käsesorten	Selection of cheeses
Nachtisch	*Dessert*
Vanille Eiscreme	Vanilla ice cream

Bruno ordered an orangeade to go with his meal.

Then he waited. The table he had chosen had room for five: three chairs and a two-person banquette were arranged around it. Since he was feeling expansive that evening, he had sat on the banquette to get a good view of the people entering the dining room from the cabins.

As more passengers came in, it wasn't long before the empty chairs at his table were filled. They were all people with whom Bruno had conversed only in passing over the previous two days.

The first to take a seat was Baroness Fridegunde van Hattem. Although her age was a state secret, a glance at her passport would have revealed that she was fifty-four years old. Build: medium. Face shape: oval. Eye colour: blue. Place of birth: Vienna. Occupation: *Haus- und Familienarbeit*, though she had never carried out any of the domestic duties of a housewife—she relied on the help of countless servants, all of whom had been left behind in her mansion.

The baroness had the strong, domineering personality of someone who, having been born into a good family, and having frequented high society since childhood and married well, expected to have her every whim satisfied. Her voice was slightly husky, almost masculine, the result of the many cigarettes she was in the habit of smoking in long cigarette holders and which, much to her displeasure, she had abstained from while on board the airship. It was her custom, or at least this is what she had told Bruno, to travel every year to escape the European winter, staying for long spells at the Copacabana Palace.

'I haven't seen winter for five years,' she said.

The second person to sit down was Dr Karl Kass Voegler. His passport gave his age as forty-five. Build: slender. Face shape: triangular. Eye colour: blue. Place of birth: Düsseldorf. Occupation: *Sanitätsarzt*, public health physician. His forehead was immense, an impression reinforced by his hair loss, which had left hair only on his temples. He sported the narrow 'toothbrush' moustache, trimmed at the edges, that was popular from north to south across the globe, stamped upon the lips of everyone from Chancellor Hitler to the Brazilian writer Monteiro Lobato, and, of course, Charlie Chaplin.

He somewhat resembled an actor in an expressionist film, with his fair, almost pale skin that would not fare well in the heat and Brazilian sun. His hands, with their long fingers and knobbly joints, moved across the table like a pair of trained albino spiders that scuttled to fetch him a piece of cutlery, a glass, his napkin, before dying with their legs seized up as his fist closed over the item in question.

The doctor had the hearty manner of a rousing public speaker and was travelling at the invitation of the German embassy in Brazil to take part in the Brazilian Eugenics Congress, where he was to give a lecture to the São Paulo Eugenics Society about the dangers of racial mixing to a nation's health.

'I didn't think that a country like Brazil would be so interested in the topic,' Bruno said. 'But I must confess, I know very little of her people.'

'The country is modernizing!' Baroness van Hattem said. 'Rio de Janeiro is beautiful! And they're most interested in questions of hygiene. Naturally, with the number of half-breeds there… That's why they have done so much to encourage European immigration, especially from Germany.'

'Yes, it's imperative that the nation's blood be whitened,' Dr Voegler agreed. 'That is precisely the topic I intend to expound to my Brazilian colleagues. They believe that by prohibiting the arrival of Asian and African immigrants, and encouraging that of Italians and Germans, the superiority of white over negroid blood will be sufficient to whiten the race.'

'But it isn't?' the baroness asked.

'No, of course it isn't,' Dr Voegler said. 'It's also necessary to promote eugenic awareness among young people. They must be encouraged, for example, not to marry members of inferior races and social classes, so that the pure races have more children than the degenerate ones, thus avoiding the proliferation of half-breeds.'

Chief Steward Kubis came to the table and the two ordered their drinks. The baroness asked for a gin and tonic, Dr Voegler just water.

'Of course, one must also sterilize the undesirables,' Dr Voegler continued. 'That was what I said in my correspondence with Dr Renato Kehl. The Brazilians are extremely enthusiastic about our work. I hear that a proposal is underway to insert an article into the new constitution making it the state's obligation to "encourage eugenic education". That is, if it hasn't already been done. I don't follow Brazilian politics.'

'And how exactly does one encourage that?' asked Bruno, more out of politeness than interest, since his attention had been captured by someone asking if the remaining chair was free. 'Of course, make yourself comfortable,' he urged the newcomer.

'By sponsoring beauty contests, for example,' Dr Voegler explained, immediately turning to the new arrival.

The young man who had sat down between them was blessed with an athletic build and Apollonian beauty, the kind only found in fashion shoots and on nationalist posters. He demanded attention, and he seemed to know it.

'Dr Voegler, baroness. What a pleasant evening, isn't it just?' he remarked, taking his seat. 'Why, sir, we have not yet been introduced. Charmed, I'm sure. I'm Mr Hay. William Hay. But you can call me Willy.'

A peek at his passport would have revealed his age to be twenty-seven. Build: slender. Face shape: square. Eye colour: brown. Place of birth: London. Occupation: (blank). He had the bold, louche gaze of a silent film lead and, as they would soon discover, the irony-laden, sharp and debonair humour of the high-born Englishman, fed from the cradle with the belief that, no matter where he went, he carried the burden of representing the only civilized society imaginable. Chief Steward Kubis came over to the table to ask what he would like to drink.

'What meat are we having today…? Ah, veal,' Mr Hay said. 'That calls for a good white wine. Bring me the Puligny-Montrachet. Will you join me?'

'I never drink,' Dr Voegler said, indicating his glass of water.

'I will, Mr Hay, don't you worry, just as soon as I finish my gin and tonic,' the baroness said.

Bruno nodded too, and Mr Hay ordered the wine.

'Forgive me, I interrupted your conversation,' Mr Hay said. 'What were you talking about?'

'About the ideal proportions of beauty,' said the baroness, with an ingratiating smile. 'A topic with which you will surely be familiar.'

'Ah yes, naturally,' he said, turning to the others. 'Yesterday at breakfast, Baroness van Hattem and I were conversing about art. I studied History of Art at Cambridge, and the baroness, from what I know, is an avid collector.'

'Of what kind of art, baroness?' Bruno asked.

'The only true kind,' she said. 'Not the sordid, degenerate paintings that pass for art these days. Quite simply sickening! Cubism, impressionism, surrealism, dadaism, it doesn't matter what "ism" they call it, it's always so sordid. And there's always a Jew behind it! *Ein Skandal!*'

'I see. What's the problem with Jews and art?'

'Everything they do is horrifying and distorted,' the baroness said.

'Yes, only racially pure artists can produce healthy art,' Dr Voegler clarified, 'art that sustains the eternal ideas of classical beauty.'

'Ah, yes, *classical* beauty,' Mr Hay said enthusiastically. 'I don't understand why they can't simply carry on painting beautiful realistic portraits, the way they used to. These days the classical forms have been twisted and deformed, and they call that art? Modernism is a disease if you ask me, an artistic aberration. Look at Picasso: his early works were perfectly acceptable, I suppose. But now you look at one of his paintings and you can't tell if you're viewing a face from the front or the side; most likely it's both at the same time. It's completely unprecedented. Or take Chagall: have a look at any one of his grotesque paintings and tell me it's not a window into the soul of the Jewish race? What is the meaning of all those dark, shady figures? To turn the negro into our racial ideal? Even Van Gogh, who has now come to be seen as a great genius, despite his crude scrawlings… nature seen through the eyes of a sick mind. Has madness itself now become a method? Pfff!' He let out a sigh and, noticing there was a man standing by his side, turned to face him. 'Don't you agree?'

Bruno, who was dividing his attention between the menu and the conversation, smiled as he recognized the man to be the very same German he had spotted in the hotel in Recife. Oval face, grey eyes, heavy bags under them, a shiny forehead that looked like it had been polished. This time, he noticed that the man also had a swastika pin on his lapel. The new arrival pointed to the empty space on the banquette next to Bruno.

'Would you mind if I sat next to you?' the German asked, speaking in a Munich accent.

'Of course not,' Bruno said, moving up for him. 'Mr...?'

'Klein,' the man introduced himself. 'Otto Klein.'

'Pleased to meet you. I'm Bruno Brückner. This is Baroness van Hattem, Dr Voegler and Mr Hay, who is English. Make yourself comfortable, Herr Klein. You boarded at Recife, did you not? I believe I saw you in the hotel restaurant, but I don't remember seeing you on board prior to that.'

'I did indeed board at Recife,' he said, sitting down next to Bruno. 'I have business in Buenos Aires, and I intended to travel by train to Rio and then continue by plane to Argentina. But when I saw that the date coincided with the arrival of the Zeppelin, I thought, "Why not?" I've never flown on an airship before.'

'What line of business are you in, Herr Klein?' Mr Hay asked.

'Coffee importation,' Otto Klein said.

'Ah, what a coincidence. My own family has been in that business for a number of years, as Hay & Sons. Perhaps you've even met my father, Douglas Hay, who—'

'Oh no, no. I've only just started working in the field. I have a contract with the German government to supply coffee to the army.'

'Really? How fortunate. What was your business before?'

Otto Klein appeared mildly distressed by the question.

'I owned a small emporium in Munich...'

Nothing further needed to be said, for everyone understood. The baroness reacted to this with raised eyebrows and a cold expression, the natural disdain felt by old money towards the nouveau riche. A change of government always creates opportunities, but it was strange, thought Bruno, that a small-time merchant from Munich, a man like Otto Klein, common and mediocre in equal measure, should suddenly be in the possession of generous government supply contracts. This fact in itself must have already opened up lines of credit for him with many banks. Otto Klein seemed to sense the baroness's disdain; he looked ill at ease, removed from his natural environment.

He started when he heard the cork pop. Chief Steward Kubis began to serve the wine, and Mr Hay offered a glass to Herr Klein.

'I wasn't aware that this flight was going to Buenos Aires,' Bruno said, changing the subject.

'The one we're on isn't,' the baroness explained. 'The Zeppelin only goes to Argentina twice a year. At other times there's an air connection in Rio de Janeiro, with the Condor Syndicate.'

When the food had been served and everyone had unfolded their napkin and tied it around their neck, the baroness took the opportunity to ask Kubis to bring her another gin and tonic. Bruno noticed that she had hardly touched her wine.

'Now, what were we discussing before Herr Klein's arrival? It was something interesting…' said the baroness, who obviously did not include Otto Klein's business in her list of interesting subjects.

'Degenerate art. And Jews,' said Bruno, who turned to Otto Klein. 'I assume you're not one of those modern artists?'

'Or a Jew,' Mr Hay joked.

'My… how absurd! Of course not!' Klein seemed nervous and agitated at the mere possibility they might consider he belonged to either category. 'To question the purity of my...'

'Easy, Herr Klein,' said Bruno, laughing. 'Mr Hay is just teasing you. His subtle English humour tends to go over the heads of us Germans...'

'Indeed, I was only joking, old fellow,' Mr Hay said.

Otto Klein let out a grunt, and the silence which then dominated the table, though largely motivated by the hunger which had made the diners turn their attention to their plates, became another source of distress for the recent arrival.

A little later, when the chief steward himself came to gather the plates and ask if he could serve dessert, they all answered yes.

'Anyway, to return to our previous discussion,' Mr Hay began, 'as much as I share your distaste for modern art, baroness, isn't it enough just to ignore it? Starve it of attention?'

'Tolerance of degenerates can be dangerous, Mr Hay, especially in the arts,' said Dr Voegler. 'I know many will think, "It's only a picture, just a drawing, nothing more," but if we continue down that road who knows where we'll end up... We must take a stand, pick a side. And I, along with many Germans, showed in the voting booths that a side has been chosen, a side with beliefs, values and ideals. The ideals of Nazism.'

'And you, my dear baroness?' said Mr Hay, turning to her. 'As a collector and patroness of the arts, how do you see the future of art in Germany?'

'Ah, I agree with what Minister Goebbels said in May. German art in the next decade must be heroic, uncompromisingly romantic, objective and unsentimental. It needs to be essential and linked to the aspirations of our people, or else it will amount to nothing. I really don't understand what the problem is with simply painting in the realist mode, as in the past.' The steward placed the bowls of vanilla ice cream on the table. The baroness continued: 'As you yourself said, Mr Hay, whatever happened to make these artists stop painting beautiful realistic paintings almost overnight?'

'Photography, perhaps?' said Bruno, with a touch of unexpected irony.

The baroness clicked her tongue and shrugged.

Then she looked at her ice cream and said:

'Oh, I think you have taken my dessert spoon, Mr Hay.'

'No, this one's mine,' the Englishman said. 'Perhaps it fell under the table? Let me see... Oh yes. There it is, by Herr Klein's feet.'

The others all leant back to look beneath the table.

'Allow me, baroness. I think I can reach it,' said Otto Klein.

He bent down to get the spoon, but Dr Voegler had already summoned Kubis.

'Please don't trouble yourself, sir,' Kubis said. 'Allow me.'

'There's no need, I've got it. Here,' Otto Klein said, lifting up the spoon, as if it were Excalibur itself in the hands of the Lady of the Lake, and handing it to the chief steward, who went off to get another one for the baroness.

'While you're at it, bring me another gin and tonic, will you?' the baroness asked.

The others began to eat their ice cream.

'Anyway, as we were saying,' the baroness continued, 'I am eagerly awaiting the restoration of classical values, so that art will go back to being beautiful and moral, as it should be.'

'Absolutely,' Mr Hay agreed. 'I am an aesthete, a great appreciator of the classical ideals of beauty, especially the Greco-Roman....' He swiftly added: 'I must admit, the restoration of the classical ideals, outdoor physical exercise, an emphasis on a virile, healthy body moulded by bucolic life... there is value in that.'

'My dear sir, if only you were German, you would be a beautiful example of the Aryan race,' Dr Voegler said. 'I can tell just by looking at you that there's not a drop of impurity in your blood.'

'Is that so?' Mr Hay asked. 'You really think it's possible to make such an analysis just by looking at someone? So, tell us, is Herr Klein here off the hook too?'

'Is that another one of your jokes, Mr Hay?' Otto Klein grunted. 'Remind us when we're meant to laugh.'

'You shouldn't let yourself be upset by such a puerile remark,' Bruno said. 'There's no call for that…'

Otto Klein noisily dropped his spoon into the bowl and glowered at his neighbour.

Then his eyebrows furrowed in curiosity.

'Sir… your face is familiar. Have we met before?'

'It's strange you should ask,' Bruno said, settling back into his seat. 'Because a few hours ago, when I saw you in the hotel in Recife, I wondered the same thing. But given my line of work, people aren't usually pleased when I recognize them.'

'Why? What is your profession?' Otto Klein asked.

'I'm a police detective in Berlin,' he said with a smile.

A look of guilty discomfort flashed across Otto Klein's face. Not that this alone could mean very much: the sober elegance of the uniforms Hugo Boss had designed for the Nazis concealed the fact that many who had been young during the Weimar period had dissolute pasts.

Otto Klein finished his ice cream in silence. He seemed to grow more uncomfortable by the minute, until finally he took his leave, claiming a sudden migraine, and announced he would be repairing to his cabin. Dr Voegler rose from his chair, allowing Klein to get up from the banquette upon which he now seemed somewhat cornered, and gave him an affable pat on the shoulder as he passed.

As soon as Klein left the dining room, the baroness was the first to lean over the table and murmur in a confidential tone:

'What a strange fellow, don't you think?'

'How does someone go from being a lowly merchant to a large-scale importer from one minute to the next?' Mr Hay asked. 'If he really is who he claims to be…'

'A lot has happened this year, with the new government,' Bruno said. 'But on the passenger manifest he is listed as "merchant", with no more detail than that.'

'A merchant… That's so vague it could mean practically anything,' Mr Hay said.

'A smuggler, even,' Dr Voegler pointed out.

'Do you think he could be some kind of criminal?' the baroness asked, turning to Bruno in a state of something closer to excitement than fear. 'Like in those books by that English writer, the one who wrote *Die Frau im Kimono*… I forget her name.'

'Who knows?' Bruno found the idea entertaining. 'But if he is a crook, he must be a very successful one if he can afford an airship ticket.'

'A smuggler, like I said,' Dr Voegler said.

'Of jewels,' Mr Hay offered, like in a guessing game.

'Jews are very skilled at handling jewels,' the baroness pointed out.

'He was looking at me awfully strangely,' Mr Hay said. 'You don't suppose he could be a… *degenerate*, do you? I met one of them in Berlin, an activist in some institute… Oh, what was the name again?'

'Dr Hirschfeld?' Dr Voegler suggested, with clear disgust in his voice.

'No, no. It was a journalist. Willer! Kurt Willer!' Mr Hay cried triumphantly.

'It makes no difference,' Dr Voegler said with a shrug. 'These degenerates from the Institut für Sexualwissenschaft are all alike. I'm proud to be able to say that I personally urged the authorities to close that place and burn all their books. We must purge Germany of this plague. It is *undeutsch*, and incompatible with National Socialism.'

'Then again, if the idea is to restore classical culture,' said Mr Hay, once more adopting a provocative tone, 'I don't see what can be more classical than "Greek love", as Gide would call it.'

Bruno and the baroness let out a chuckle.

'I shall forgive that joke, Mr Hay,' Dr Voegler said. 'However, in this case the issue is not "aesthetic" in nature; rather it has to do with the most pragmatic eugenics. Behaviour that does not enable the reproduction of the human race cannot be accepted. Besides, these degenerates are mostly Jews. Worse than that, they're Jews and communists.'

'Oh, the communists!' hissed the baroness, with a shudder of genuine hatred. For the first time she seemed agitated. 'Like the Jew Marx! The Bolsheviks were all Jews too, did you know that? Yes, it's true, my friend Gertrud heard it from a cousin who learnt it from someone who knew an official who served in the White Army! The Jews killed the Tsar and came to Germany to poison our civil servants with those odious unions of theirs! My poor Helmut became ill from all those strikes, those senseless demands! With all the jobs he created in these crisis-stricken times, you'd expect them to be more grateful, but nothing of the sort... the unions corrupted them. I remember when Herr Goering invited my husband and other entrepreneurs to come and meet their candidate before the election. No one wanted more elections, but Helmut came back the picture of contentment, most relieved, in fact, saying that if the Nazis won a parliamentary majority, they might be the last elections for a good ten years... but now I pray it's a hundred!'

The baroness spoke of her husband in a boastful way, namedropping to give more weight to her husband's social status.

'Anyone who was anyone was there. Krupp, Siemens, Opel, Allianz, BMW, Daimler-Benz... and my Helmut, of course,' she said, mentioning the names with a feigned carelessness, carefully calculated to impress. 'And everyone agreed when Hitler said it was impossible for private enterprise to be maintained in a democracy. That it was necessary to do away with the unions, allow each boss to be a... a... a *Führer* in their own company. And that was music to our ears. Everyone was relieved. I told Helmut: that man will save the Germanic race from the threat of Jewish communism. That's why we donated so generously to the campaign.'

'Tell me, my dear Dr Voegler,' asked Mr Hay, 'as an expert, do you think our friend Otto Klein over there'—he glanced over at the empty space—'could be a Jew?'

'If that really is his name,' the baroness added.

Dr Voegler took a sip of water and stroked his chin.

'Perhaps... I didn't want to say anything at the time so as not to upset anyone, but I did detect certain Hebraic traits. And if he is a Jew then he is certainly a communist. Mr Hay, are you familiar with our *Myth*?'

'Are you referring to that book, what was it called?' Mr Hay said.

'Precisely. *The Myth of the Twentieth Century*, by Rosenberg. It's the fundamental work of the Nazi truth. It exposes the folly of professional philosophers in seeking a "unique and eternal" truth using reason and explains how God created humanity in a racial hierarchy, making the Nordic Aryans its elite. That's why communists are our greatest threat. They stand for a society in which all would be treated as equals, leaving the Aryan races at the mercy of the Semites, making it easier for the Jews to put their plan for global domination into action, which—'

'Honestly, Rosenberg's worldview is rather mystical for my taste,' Mr Hay said. 'Besides, "the folly of the professional philosophers" sounds slightly resentful, don't you think? I know he didn't study philosophy, but—'

'If you will allow me, ladies and gentlemen, I too shall bid you goodnight,' Bruno said. Having already finished his dessert, he removed the napkin from his neck, wiped his lips and dropped it onto the table.

He left the dining room and went down the corridor to his cabin. The back of the sofa had been folded out into a bed. He was delighted at the thought of sleeping alone, spared a roommate's inevitable snoring. He looked out of the window one last time but was unable to see much beyond the ocean. He took off his suit and put his pyjamas on, then lay down to sleep the sleep of the just.

Three

BRUNO Brückner thought he could hear distant, muffled shouts and opened his eyes. He got up, looked out of the window and saw that it was still dark. They were flying quite low and the gleam of nearby lights was visible below. The voices were coming from the outside, beneath him: the mail sacks, brought from Europe via Zeppelin, were being flung out onto an airfield. He went back to bed.

He was woken again by daylight shining through the window—he had left the curtains open for that very reason. He liked to rise early and be the first to use the washroom and the men's WC. He put his slippers on, exited the cabin and crossed the corridor to the stern, in the direction of the lavatory. Occupied. The doors to the two WCs, it occurred to him, were the only ones on the airship that locked from the inside.

He looked both ways down the narrow corridor that ran between the cabins, silent except for the buzzing of the rotors and the distant clanking of cutlery in the galley. He couldn't see anyone.

He tried the door to the ladies' lavatory: open. He went in, urinated and pulled the flush. The waste, he later discovered, was simply dropped from the airship when they were over the ocean. He walked to one of the washrooms. They were the same size as the cabins, but without a sofa bed taking up half the room, they seemed far more spacious. Bruno enjoyed having all that space to himself for a moment. He washed his face, brushed his teeth and dried his hands on the towel.

When he left, out of curiosity he checked the door to the men's lavatory again. Still locked. He put his ear to the door but heard nothing.

As he went back along the corridor he noticed that one of the cabin doors was open. He didn't know whose cabin it was, but he assumed its occupant was currently in the men's lavatory. He peeped inside, saw that the room was empty, and closed the door.

Putting the matter aside, he returned to his cabin and devoted himself to the process of changing out of his pyjamas and into his suit. Tucking the tails of his shirt inside his trousers, he pulled his braces over his shoulders and let them snap into place. He did up his tie, put on his waistcoat and jacket, and looked in his briefcase for the swastika pin to reattach to his lapel.

Then he picked up his copy of the only book of Brazilian literature he had found in the bookshops of Berlin, *Geschichten aus Rio de Janeiro* by Machado de Assis, and sat down to read some stories.

An hour later, Bruno Brückner entered the dining room, empty except for him, but with the cutlery and china already laid out.

'*Guten Morgen,* Herr Brückner,' Chief Steward Kubis greeted him.

'Good morning,' Bruno said, turning the chair around before taking a seat, in order to have a good view of the window. They were passing over a large city. 'Do you know which city we passed just before dawn? Where the mail sacks were thrown out?'

'I think it was Salvador da Bahia, but I can check with the commander. Would you like your breakfast now, sir?'

'Yes please.'

Bread, freshly baked on board, butter, honey and jams, boiled eggs served in porcelain *coquetiers*, ham, salami, cheese and fruit were brought to the table. Coffee or tea? Bruno ordered coffee, with a little milk and some cocoa powder to help his digestion throughout the day. The heavy white porcelain of the teapot, milk jug and the spoons bore the letters 'LZ', the initials of the airline, with blue stripes and gold borders. He picked up the spoon and carried out a delicate lobotomy on the egg, tapping it lightly to break the top of the shell and slicing off a layer of firm, smooth white to reveal the still-soft yolk inside it. He sprinkled on a little salt and pepper and ate.

He gave himself over to enjoying his breakfast, having the whole room to himself, the silence broken only by the electrical buzzing of the propellers, which were turned on at times when the air currents alone were not sufficient to push the airship along. He spent an hour this way, while the other passengers gradually appeared in the dining room.

Bruno looked outside again. He concluded that the experience of being on the airship was similar to spending the whole day at the cinema, watching a silent, plotless film being projected onto the windows—which made him remember with fondness the last film he had seen in Berlin.

He contemplated the gold-rimmed spoon. The wing illustration and the blue line against the white porcelain gave it an air of Greek ceramics. As luxurious as the experience was, it was a claustrophobic kind of luxury. He could hardly wait to walk about in the open, with the sky above his head.

Kubis came over to him.

'The commander has informed me that it was indeed Salvador. Now we're approaching Ilhéus, *mein Herr*.'

A Brazilian lady on another table called the chief steward over and made a complaint in Portuguese. Bruno found the accent curious; the faster and more open way they spoke was different from the Portuguese he had come across in Berlin. From what he gleaned from the conversation, which was speckled with the odd German word, he could partly make out the nature of the complaint: the gentlemen were using the ladies' lavatory. The man with her made an embarrassed confession, only to be reprimanded by his wife.

Kubis nodded to the couple, and before he left the room, Bruno waved at him.

'Is it by any chance to do with the gents' WC?' he murmured.

'Yes,' the chief steward said. 'She's complaining that the men on board are using the ladies' lavatory, because someone is locked inside the gents.'

'How strange. I woke up very early, and even then the door was already locked. Perhaps it's just stuck?'

'We'll check right away, sir.'

Kubis rushed out of the dining room into the corridor, passing Dr Voegler, who was coming in the opposite direction, from his cabin. As soon as he saw Bruno

Brückner, Dr Voegler nodded and joined him at his table, bidding him good morning. A mug awaited him, and he poured himself some coffee.

'I'm sorry to have left you so early last night, doctor,' Bruno apologized, 'but I'm in the habit of waking early, and I was dead tired. The discussion was very interesting and instructive, however. Did I miss much?'

'Ah, no, not a great deal, Herr Brückner.' The doctor took a sausage and cut it in half. 'Except for a demonstration of Baroness van Hattem's surprising tolerance for alcohol. She ordered two more gin and tonics, can you believe it? She drank them like water.'

'I think we shall soon discover the results.'

The next familiar face to appear in the dining room was that of Mr Hay, who came and sat down next to them and asked for tea.

'Gentlemen, I trust you both had a good night's sleep?' he said. 'I can't say so myself, I'm afraid, what with all that commotion.'

'What commotion?' Bruno asked.

'That shouting outside as they were throwing down the mail bundles. Then all the people striding up and down the corridor. If you'll allow me to make a criticism, my dear sirs, you Germans don't know how to walk. All you do is march. Such heavy footsteps!'

'Is that so? The mail being thrown down, I remember

hearing that,' Bruno said. 'But footsteps in the corridors, no. However, I am a deep sleeper.'

Just then, Kubis came hurrying through the dining room towards the prow, pale-faced and seemingly in great distress—a passenger asking for more coffee was completely ignored.

'I say, is something the matter?'

'I believe there's a problem with the men's WC.'

'Ah, so it wasn't just me. I tried to use it and it was occupied,' Mr Hay said. And then, in a quieter voice: 'I ended up using the ladies.'

'I woke up early and had the same problem,' Bruno said. 'But that was more than two hours ago. It can't be the same person inside.'

'Perhaps the door's jammed,' Mr Hay suggested.

'That's what I said to Kubis.'

'Well, it wasn't jammed when I used it in the middle of the night,' Dr Voegler said.

'Really,' Bruno said, intrigued. 'What time was that?'

'Oh, just after the mail packages were thrown out. Perhaps I was one of the men who woke you with my heavy German steps, Mr Hay. I'm sorry if I interrupted your sleep.'

'Don't worry, my dear fellow,' Mr Hay reassured him. 'It's hardly a matter of life or death.'

Kubis hurried through the dining room again, heading from the prow to the cabins, this time accompanied by three mechanics, one of whom stationed himself at the entrance to the corridor, as if to stop anyone else going that way. The chief steward, visibly distressed, busied himself with attending to the passengers in the room, filling their pots with more coffee, tea or cocoa, fetching more bread and jam… Noticing that something was amiss, Mr Hay asked what was, as he had discovered for himself, the most frequently repeated question in Germany:

'Is everything in order?'

'A minor inconvenience, gentlemen. It's being resolved as we speak.'

Some more minutes passed until the mechanics returned from the cabins. One of them whispered into the ear of Kubis, who nodded and left the dining room, headed once more for the prow. He promptly returned, and, walking over to the table at which Bruno, Mr Hay and Dr Voegler were having their breakfast, awkwardly cleared his throat.

'Herr Brückner, the commander would like to talk to you alone.'

'Something wrong?' Bruno asked.

'Oh, not at all!' Kubis glanced anxiously about the room, failing to conceal his nerves. Whatever it was, he didn't want the other passengers to hear. 'Well, it's simply a… consultation, so to speak. Of course, if it's not inconvenient…'

'Not at all. At your service.'

'Please, come with me.'

They left the dining room for the prow. The prow corridor was L-shaped, with the passageway to starboard leading to the galley door and ending at the entrance to the gondola. Ahead, the corridor passed the door to the radio room to port before ending in the navigation cabin, which stretched all the way from one side of the gondola to the other. On the port side there was a small desk, along with a table and chair, a nautical map of the Atlantic Ocean and a ladder that led up to the airship's interior. On the starboard side there was a fold-down table and a bed for the commander. But the commander was nowhere to be seen. Bruno followed Kubis through yet another door to the *Steuerraum*, the command deck.

The semicircular cabin's outer walls were set with large windows, with the wheel controlling the ship's rudder in the middle, between two iron girders set in a V shape. The view from the windows was magnificent. Above, the milky-white clouds were like a moving mountain range. Below, the city and the fields were a world in miniature, an architect's model brought to life by a fairy-tale spell.

There with his back to them, holding a cup of tea in his hands, intent upon the helmsman before him at the wheel, was Count Ferdinand von Zeppelin's successor as director of LZ; this was the man who had trained all the German airship pilots during the Great War, who had managed to make the Americans fold and allow the building of new German airships after the defeat, and who had managed to have them built without resorting to government money; the man who led the first round-the-world trip on an airship, the first Arctic flight, and the electrifying first Zeppelin journey across Brazil, years earlier: Commander Hugo Eckener.

He had a long face, with deep crows' feet around his weary eyes and big bags beneath them. A greying moustache and goatee framed a small, severe mouth, and his hair was cut very short so that it stood on end, making him look as if he had had an electric shock. He looked Bruno up and down as if trying to get the measure of him. When the commander's eyes fixed on the lapel pin, his gaze hardened and his lips pursed in disgust at the sight of the swastika.

Bruno cleared his throat uncomfortably. Of course, he thought to himself, he had forgotten a notorious and widely known detail about Commander Eckener: he *detested* Nazis. He had detested them from the very beginning, when the press and the political establishment considered them just a histrionic joke, something not to be taken seriously. And he never hesitated to criticize their authoritarian economic policies, their persecution of minorities, Germany's slide towards autocracy... Above all, he hated Chancellor Adolf Hitler.

It was said that the feeling was mutual. Hugo Eckener was a national hero, and God forbid anyone should shine more brightly in the eyes of the German people than the Führer. Even worse, during the 1932 electoral campaign, Eckener had been sounded out by both the left-wing social democrats and the *Zentrum* as a unity candidate against the right, which was led by the Nazis. In the end he refused, but the antipathy remained: he did not let the Nazis use Zeppelin hangars for their rallies and rejected any attempt by Minister Goebbels to use their airships as propaganda for the current government. Nor was it any secret that the Nazis were out to harm him in any way they could, as they grew more powerful and placed their followers in positions of influence.

'Herr Brückner,' the commander said, 'in our entire history of commercial flights, no Luftschiffbau Zeppelin passenger has ever suffered anything worse than a bump on the head from falling out of bed or a burnt tongue from drinking their coffee too hot. "Safety first" has always been and shall continue to be our motto, and I have already gone against governors and directors to ensure it stays that way.' He took a final sip of his tea and handed the cup to the chief steward. 'However, something happened early this morning. Something which leads us to believe that a crime has taken place. I do not, however, intend to give you lot any reason to use this against my airline.'

'You lot… What do you mean by that?' Bruno asked.

The commander pointed at the party pin on his suit.

'Oh, I see…' Bruno said. 'I understand your misgivings, commander. But you must realize, not all those who support the Nazis do it because they agree with their attacks on the Jews, their authoritarianism or their paranoid theories about the "stab-in-the-back" conspiracy. Many of those who voted for Hitler were simply tired of the rampant corruption of the Weimar system and wanted a change in direction for Germany.'

Upon hearing this, the young helmsman interrupted.

'There's a word for those people too.'

'Is there really? What is it?'

'Nazis,' he said gruffly.

Bruno remained impassive, staring at the boy. Knut Eckener, the son of the commander, and the Zeppelin's helmsman, stared back at him defiantly, his lips pursed in a glare which mingled suppressed rage with deep disdain.

Now it was Commander Eckener's turn to sigh.

'Don't get involved, Knut,' he said. 'I'm afraid my son's opinions are even sterner than mine. In any case, you're a police officer in Berlin, correct?' he asked.

'Yes, I'm a police detective.'

'Then allow me to lay out the situation for you: a person has died on board. His body was found in the men's WC and discreetly carried back to his cabin while the other passengers were having their breakfast. Why, or in what circumstances he came to perish, we do not know.'

'There's a doctor on board, Dr Klaus Voegler. He could—'

Eckener raised his hand, interrupting him. 'Yes, I'm aware of that. But I have reasons for not wanting to involve Dr Voegler in this. There are other complications.'

'What are they?'

'The victim was carrying two passports.'

'The "victim"? Do you think he was murdered?'

'Given that one of the passports is in a completely different name from the one with which he embarked, and taking the other name into account, it's a possibility. But understand, Herr Brückner, that it's not only my company's reputation that's at stake. The death took place on Brazilian soil. Or, rather, above it. So, one must also bear in mind how uncomfortable it would be to submit our passengers, among whom are numbered the cream of Brazilian and German society, to police interrogations. Some of them, I believe, are early supporters and funders of your party, which could also create diplomatic awkwardness.'

'I see. And how would you like to resolve matters?'

'Well…' Commander Eckener pondered for a moment. 'Tell me, would you be able to tell a genuine passport from a forgery?'

'Actually, yes, I would. It's part of the job these days.'

'We reach Rio de Janeiro tonight. If, when we dock, we already have as many answers as possible, that will make things a little easier.'

'I will do what I can to help, commander.'

'In that case, in the name of Luftschiffbau Zeppelin, I thank you in advance, and I apologize for the inconvenience we are causing you on your journey. If you ever intend to travel with us again, I shall have the greatest pleasure in—'

'There's no need, commander,' Bruno reassured him. 'To be honest, there's not a great deal to do during the journey. I'd be glad of the distraction.'

'Well, in that case, Chief Steward Kubis will take you to the victim's cabin, and you can enlighten us as to the occupant's true identity.'

Bruno nodded. He followed Kubis back through the ship, until the two stopped in front of the last starboard door before the washroom. After checking that there were no other passengers nearby, he opened the door and they entered.

'*Mein Gott!*' Bruno said.

There, laid out on the bed, was the body of Otto Klein.

He was in pyjamas, his mouth and eyes open and frozen in an expression of deep anguish and despair. His hands clutched at his chest and his fingers were rigid, like claws, as if, in his last moment spent gasping for air, his entire body had set about reproducing Munch's *The Scream*. It was a terrifying sight.

Kubis related how, as the lavatory door had been locked from inside, he had used his master key to get in. When he found Otto Klein slumped on the floor, he had tried to stay calm—in his many years working in the best hotels in Europe he'd seen it all—and, once he had checked that the passenger was dead and nothing could be done for him, he had immediately alerted the commander.

'You acted correctly, Chief Steward Kubis,' Bruno said, walking over to the desk where the deceased had left some papers. 'Are these the passports?'

'Yes.'

Bruno inspected them.

The first gave the name Otto Klein. From the date of birth, he calculated his age to be thirty years. Build:

medium. Face shape: oval. Eye colour: grey. Place of birth: Munich. Occupation: merchant.

On the second passport, however, the photograph had been removed, and there was a completely different name: Jonas Shmuel Kurtzberg. Twenty-six. Build: medium. Face shape: oval. Eye colour: grey. Place of birth: Hamburg. Occupation: *Porträtfotograf.* Portrait photographer.

Bruno understood the commander's hesitation now. The victim was a Jew.

'What do we know about him?' he asked.

'He boarded in Recife with the name Otto Klein on his *Reisepass*,' Kubis said. 'And he remained in his cabin until supper. He also retired early. The only people who spoke to him were those he dined with. I believe you were at the same table, sir.'

'I was, yes. But we didn't end up talking much,' Bruno said. 'Mr Hay provoked him with a stupid joke, and he was greatly troubled by the mere suggestion that he might be Jewish. Ah... wait.'

Bruno sniffed the air as if he were following a scent. He approached the bed and bent over the body, seeming to smell it; then he grunted pensively and stroked his chin.

'What is it?' the chief steward asked. 'Something out of the ordinary?'

'Yes, haven't you noticed?'

'What?'

'The smell. Like bitter almonds.'

The steward came closer to the body and gave the air a tentative sniff. Then he immediately clapped his hand to his mouth in shock. He had read enough detective novels to know what that meant.

'Tell the commander that we know one thing for certain,' Bruno said. 'This death was not due to natural causes.'

Four

I N the *Steuerraum*, hovering over the miniaturized world beneath them, Bruno laid out his conclusions to Commander Eckener.

'These are small details, commander, but they leap out to trained eyes,' Bruno explained, showing him the passports. 'If you look carefully, you'll see that on the chief of police's stamp, the words *Polizeipräsident* and *München* are normally separated by four dots, forming a small square. It's like that on any passport. On Otto Klein's, however, you'll notice the words are separated by six dots. It is, therefore, a false stamp on a false passport. I am led, then, to believe that the man's true name was in fact Jonas Kurtzberg.'

The commander looked at both passports. He had never paid attention to that level of detail, and he wondered how many fake passports might already have passed through his hands.

'What about the cause of death?'

'Cyanide, commander,' Bruno explained. 'A rather dangerous poison, which can kill within seconds if a large dose is taken, or over several hours in smaller doses. The symptoms are dizziness, dry mouth… and vomiting. That would explain why Herr Klein—or should I say Herr Kurtzberg?—went to the lavatory. But then he got dizzy, fell and lost consciousness before suffocating. However, I believe you already suspected as much, did you not?'

He carefully observed Commander Eckener's reaction.

'Indeed,' Bruno said, unsurprised. 'Is that why you didn't want to involve Dr Voegler?'

'Maybe.'

'Do you suspect him?'

'I wouldn't go that far. But I wouldn't discount the possibility, given the dead man's true identity. That's why I thought to consult you first.'

'Couldn't he have committed suicide?' suggested Knut, over at the rudder wheel.

'Well, it seems to me that, if he wanted to kill himself, he would have done it before boarding,' Bruno said. 'I don't see why anyone would plan to commit suicide on board a Zeppelin, mid-journey. Unless he felt he was about to be discovered. It's certainly possible; he was rather nervous when his Hebraic origins were suggested at dinner. But we're in Brazil, not Germany. He'd have had no problems upon disembarking. Therefore suicide is out of the question. Now, from my experience... thank you, Kubis,' he said as he took the cup of coffee the chief steward handed to him, 'this kind of crime, in these circumstances, can have only two possible motives: to silence someone before they talk or to exact revenge for some past misdeed. Which leads me to believe that someone on board recognized him.'

'I recall that he was the last passenger to board at Recife, sir,' said Kubis.

'And did you notice anything strange?' Bruno asked.

'No. He looked excited about the journey, like everyone boarding with us for the first time. But he spent a long time in his cabin, then he was one of the last to enter the dining room and one of the first to retire to bed. As I told you, the only people who conversed with him were those seated at that table: Mr William Hay, Dr Karl Voegler, Baroness Fridegunde van Hattem, and, of course, you, sir.'

'You're forgetting one person, Kubis.'

'Who?'

'You.' Bruno smiled and immediately reassured the chief steward, who had inhaled sharply, like an indignant blowfish. 'Easy, my good man. I have no reason to suspect your testimony. But you did in fact *converse* with him, even if it was only to serve him at dinner, and it was you who found the body and led the efforts to remove it from the crime scene. In an ordinary police inquiry, I would have to take a statement from you. Speaking of which, I will need a discreet location in which to take statements. Are there any unoccupied cabins? That's the second thing that must be done.'

'The cabin next to the ladies' lavatory is empty,' the commander said. 'But what's the first thing?'

'To check the victim's personal baggage. There may be something in his belongings that will give us some clue. Naturally, commander, I shall require your permission for this.'

'I'll come with you,' Commander Eckener announced.

However, returning to the dining room while keeping up appearances was no simple matter. The commander first spoke to each passenger, asking them how they were enjoying the flight, whether their lodgings were acceptable and if they'd had a good night's sleep, while Bruno, having slipped back down the corridor to the cabins, waited outside the room of the late Otto Klein/Jonas Kurtzberg.

Once he had dispensed with his duties, the commander joined Bruno, and the two men were finally able to enter the cabin. At the sight of the body, Eckener gasped and stopped in his tracks.

'Is this the first dead body you've seen?' Bruno asked.

'No. I mean, yes, in these circumstances. A murdered man…'

'But during the war, I imagine…'

'I wasn't allowed to go to the front,' Eckener said. 'The Kaiser said I was too valuable as a pilot instructor to run the risk. Anyway, even if I had gone, I don't think I'd have seen much from so high up.'

'I heard the airship bombardments over London were terrible,' Bruno said. 'I believe Mr Hay talked about it at dinner.'

Bruno looked carefully at the suit hanging from the coat rack. There was a brown leather suitcase on the floor and some belongings scattered across the bedside table, including a golden swastika-shaped pin, a small key and the two passports.

'I think, if you're a Jew travelling under a German name,' Bruno said, picking up the pin and handing it to the commander, 'the best way to keep up the disguise is by taking it to the extreme. Now, let's see…'

He picked up the leather suitcase, placed it on the table and tried the key in the two locks. It opened. He raised the lid slowly. It contained photography equipment: a Leica III camera, with lenses and a few rolls of film. There was also a vial containing a blue powder.

'Ah. Ferrous ferrocyanide,' said Bruno, showing the bottle to the commander. 'Also known as "Prussian blue". Widely used in painting, but also in photography to produce cyanotypes.'

'Does this tell us anything?' Eckener asked.

'When mixed with hydrochloric acid, it produces... you guessed it: cyanide.'

'But who would bring hydrochloric acid on a journey?'

Bruno reflected upon this question for a moment.

'Hydrochloric acid is widely used to preserve food, purify water and... in many pharmaceuticals. And, as you have pointed out, sir, we have a doctor on board. Perhaps I should take a look in Dr Voegler's baggage before drawing any conclusions. Wait... what do we have here?'

At the bottom of the suitcase was a brown paper envelope. Bruno opened it. Inside were two magazines and some photos.

'Oh. I'd say this adds fuel to the fire.'

The first magazine was called *Die Insel* (The Island). On the cover was an extremely beautiful, naked young man with black hair, his beauty like that of a Greek *koûros*, facing the camera with his arms in a bodybuilder pose. His athletic, smooth body, newly entered into adulthood, gleamed with oil like the Olympian athletes of Antiquity, all the way from the hair that was glued to his head, as if it had been licked down, to the sparse hairs of his pubis, with the layout cutting off the photograph exactly where it would have begun to reveal more than decorum would allow to show on a cover, even on liberal German magazine stands. The photo credit on the following page said: 'Sent by a friend and *Die Insel* subscriber in Rio de Janeiro.'

Leafing through its pages, one could see that it contained poems, opinion pieces, political and satirical essays, and erotic, moral or romantic stories. In the editorial, it urged readers to spend their money at businesses managed *by* and *for* homosexuals, and to frequent only the bars and restaurants advertised in the magazine's pages, such as Café Dorian Gray, on 57 Bülowstraße, 'frequented by respectable homosexuals who encourage respectable behaviour, and with an honourable clientele'. There were also adverts for lesbian bars, such as Monbijou and Clube Violetta, the latter accompanied by a photograph of its patroness Lotte Hahm wearing a men's suit. There were advertisements for hotels, hairdressers, shoemakers, furniture shops and a photography studio too, which leapt to Bruno's attention: 'J. Kurtzberg—*Moderne Fotokunst*'.

All of this was interspersed with photos, lots of photos of naked young men, sometimes imitating classical poses, other times resting drowsily in rustic, painterly landscapes; sometimes smiling at the camera, or else gazing into the horizon, their bodies healthy, athletic and smooth as marble, proudly exhibiting their own nudity to the camera, as the reader's object of desire rested casually between their legs. An anecdotal essay defended the free right to masturbation, going against the received wisdom which claimed it was injurious to health. On another page, the D'Eon Transvestite Association advised so-called 'transsexuals', a term recently coined by Dr Hirschfeld for those who did not identify with their gender, about how to request their 'transvestite certificate' from the German police. Everything in the magazine had an everyday tone to it, suggesting a casual, busy social life.

The second magazine was more discreet and elitist: its cover was white, neutral, with the title *Der Eigene* (The Unique) in capital letters, followed by its designation as a 'magazine of male culture'. The content, judging by the names of those involved, was of a superior quality: the artistic nudes were done by Baron Wilhelm von Gloeden, who photographed his Italian boys from Taormina in classical dress and poses; and the literary essays were penned by Klaus Mann, with sombre and sensual illustration by Sascha Schneider. There were poems and stories written by well-respected names, a section for reviews of books of 'male interest', as well as the political manifestos of an anarchist pursuing rights for homosexuals. Everything in this magazine sounded more serious, literate and somewhat pretentious. A review of André Gide's autobiography caught his attention: it was signed by one 'W. Hay'.

'"An aesthete, a great appreciator of the classical ideals of beauty,"' Bruno said, repeating what he had heard the previous night.

'Who said that?' the commander asked.

'The English gentleman, Mr Hay, at dinner yesterday.'

Then Bruno inspected the loose photographs inside the envelope. They were less erotic and more artistic, both in their framing and in their modernistic use of light and shadow, even if the objects were the same: beautiful young men in bathing shorts, bronzing themselves under the sun on German beaches, sitting deep in reflection on lake shores like Narcissi, or rolling around in the sand in such a way that it was impossible to say whether they were embracing or mock-fighting, like puppy dogs at play. On the reverse of each photo, the names, location and date had been written.

One in particular showed a young man crouching, looking down, wearing only bathing shorts, supporting himself on a wooden post from which water was falling onto his head and streaming down his face, chin and lips—which, in the summer heat, formed an 'o' of ecstatic refreshment. When Bruno looked at the reverse of the photo, his eyes stuck out on stalks.

Meanwhile, the commander, made nervous by all of this, said:

'Please, Herr Brückner, be discreet with our passengers. He will not be the first, nor the last, of our passengers to possess the inverted inclinations of the third sex. As long as a gentleman maintains his discretion in public, this is not our business. Besides… *Scheiße.*' Bruno had shown him the back of the photograph. 'Is that the name of the boy in this photo?'

'It seems to be.'

On the back of the photograph was written: 'Fridolin van Hattem, on the shores of the Baltic Sea, 1931'.

'Degenerate art rears its ugly head,' said Bruno.

'Do you believe he is related to the baroness?'

'Perhaps. There's no way of knowing without asking her. Speaking of which…' A macabre thought had occurred to Bruno. 'I didn't see her in the lounge this morning; she didn't come in for breakfast. In fact, I haven't seen her since last night.'

The two men left the victim's cabin and made their way to the door of the baroness's cabin. They knocked and waited. No response. They opened the door to find the cabin empty. They heard a strident guffaw coming from the dining room and headed in that direction.

There was the baroness, seated at the table with Dr Voegler and Mr Hay, being served a prairie oyster—a whole egg yolk in a glass, with a dash of Worcester sauce, vinegar, table salt and black pepper, downed in one, and believed to be ideal for curing hangovers—by Kubis.

'My dear lady, you have the strength of a Valkyrie!' Dr Voegler observed.

'Don't the Valkyries come to carry the dead away?' Bruno remarked as he approached the table. 'Did you sleep well, baroness? Were you woken up by the toings and froings in the corridor?'

'I confess I am a heavy sleeper, Herr Brückner, and I did not hear anything. The constant buzzing of the propellers, I was practically mesmerized…'

Bruno nodded and glanced sideways at Kubis, who looked rather nervous standing by the table. He turned to Commander Eckener and murmured in his ear that, as it was almost time for lunch to be served, it made sense to take Kubis's statement first, so that he would be available as soon as possible to deliver the in-flight service.

'As you wish,' Commander Eckener said. 'But I want to take part in all the interrogations. I must know what goes on in my airship. Wait for me. I will give instructions to the helmsman.'

He indicated which cabin would be used and asked Bruno to wait there.

Five

CHIEF steward Heinrich Kubis was forty-six years old. He was tall, his suit always impeccable, his black hair perfectly combed and gelled with brilliantine. His references were equally impeccable: he had worked as a waiter at the Ritz in Paris and the Carlton in London. In 1912, three months before the *Titanic* sank, he began his service on the Luftschiffbau Zeppelin, a wise career move given the possible alternative. With that he had become, in practice, the world's first air steward. Everyone considered him an enchanting person, a true major-domo in the old style, still working in that agitated, post-Great War world. Not only did he have naturally good manners, but he also understood the small touches that made everything more pleasant: a bouquet of flowers, a good sauce, the exact temperature at which to serve champagne.

The chief steward was a man so devoted to pleasing his passengers that he read the society columns with the professional dedication of someone poring over fiscal balance sheets and business reports, to learn as much as he could about future guests. Holding the passenger list in his hands he was able, without any apparent need to organize his memory, to give a succinct biography of almost everyone on it, with helpful observations about their business dealings, love lives and family connections.

'...This gentleman exports coffee to France and Germany, it's his third time travelling with us... This lady is the sister of the wife of a cousin of the Brazilian president; by the way, Mr Getúlio Vargas has travelled with us before... This gentleman over here is a journalist with *The Times*; famously, Hemingway once attacked him with a shoe...'

He had been with LZ for twenty-two years now, having served on board all its commercial airships in that period. He was on LZ10 *Schwaben* when it caught fire; on LZ 13 *Hansa* when it carried out the first international flight to Copenhagen; on LZ 120 *Bodensee* when the first in-flight service was inaugurated—a beautiful airship which had to be handed over to the Italians as war reparations, and which was subsequently dismantled so that the materials could be reused.

'The brutes,' the chief steward lamented, drawing to a close the brief summary of his career. He was sitting next to Bruno on the cabin sofa, while the commander stood, looking on attentively.

'*Mein Herr*, you have no idea the things I've seen. An airship on fire above the fields of Düsseldorf. The dawn light over the New York horizon, seen from the sky. And one day, all those moments will be lost in time, like bubbles in a glass of champagne.'

'You are already part of the history of aviation, Kubis,' Bruno said.

'And I hope I will continue to be, if God wills it so. I can hardly wait to begin serving on board the new airship we're building in Hamburg. It's going to be almost as big as the *Titanic*.'

'Really? And what will its name be?' Bruno asked.

'*Hindenburg*,' Commander Eckener replied for him, 'although that is still under discussion, Herr Brückner. Your people insist that it be called *Hitler*. But I guarantee that will not happen as long as I am in charge of LZ.'

'My people? Ah, yes.' Bruno reflected for a moment, then turned back to Chief Steward Kubis. 'You had no idea that the passenger Otto Klein was actually one Jonas Kurtzberg, I suppose?' He picked up the passport and took another look at the name.

'How could I? I'd never seen him before.'

'You said he looked somewhat distressed as he was boarding, correct?'

'As I said before, so does everyone flying with us for the first time.'

'And he was one of the last to board, was he not?'

'And one of the last to enter the dining room, as I already told you. I greeted him at the entrance, confiscated all matches and lighters, as I always do, and didn't see him again until dinner in the dining room. I also noticed that he was one of the last to take his seat and one of the first to go to bed afterwards. He didn't ask for anything while he was in his cabin.'

'At what time were the mail bundles thrown down over Salvador?'

'At 4 a.m.,' Commander Eckener responded.

'I had long since retired by then,' Kubis said.

Bruno turned to the commander. 'And I imagine you wouldn't have heard the movements in the corridor.'

Bruno turned back to Kubis. 'By the way, where is your cabin located?'

'Inside the hull, with the other crew members,' Kubis said. 'Of the crew, only the commander and the helmsman sleep in the gondola—one sleeps in the navigation room while the other keeps watch on the command deck.'

Bruno then addressed the commander:

'Could a crew member have snuck into the passenger gondola at night and injected cyanide into the victim?'

'And why would a member of my crew do that?' Eckener went on the defensive. 'The only one who had any contact with the victim yesterday was Chief Steward Kubis.'

'How many men in total are there in the crew?' Bruno asked.

'Three in the passenger team, eleven in navigation, three in radio, and twenty-two in engineering. And me, obviously.'

'That makes forty people, commander,' Bruno said pensively. 'What about stowaways? Is it possible there's someone hidden away inside the ship?'

Commander Eckener and Chief Steward Kubis glanced at each other.

'There have been cases...' the commander admitted.

"I see. If there were a stowaway somewhere in the hull, could he have got into the passenger gondola without being noticed?' Bruno asked.

'There's only one entrance to the passenger gondola from inside the hull,' Kubis explained. 'A ladder in the navigation room, which is visible from the command deck, where either the commander or the helmsman is always on duty.'

'Such a stowaway could never get through the crew's sleeping quarters, and even if he did, he couldn't climb down the ladder into the gondola without my son or myself noticing,' the commander pointed out.

Bruno reflected on the matter.

'I'd like to take a look at the crew's sleeping quarters and, if you don't object, commander, ask them a few questions too.'

Eckener grunted impatiently but agreed.

'It can be done. I will accompany you myself.'

'One last question for Chief Steward Kubis, before we let him get back to his duties,' Bruno said. 'You mentioned you read the society columns to stay informed about your passengers, correct? Do you know if Baroness van Hattem has any sons?'

'Oh no, no sons. But I believe she has a nephew, Fridolin. He was engaged, but I read that it was broken off… I don't know why. Naturally, the society columns don't go into such details.'

'Certainly. Many thanks, chief steward. Now, commander, please could you lead me into the belly of this beast?'

Bruno followed Commander Eckener into the engineering room and climbed the metal ladder which led to the interior of the hull.

'Watch your step, Herr Brückner.'

'The belly of this beast' turned out to be quite apt. The airship's axial gangway, a structure shaped like an inverted triangle composed of three metallic beams, ran the length of the vast hull like a metal spine, supported at regular intervals by rib-like struts. In between were sixteen gigantic gasbags tethered by nets: the intestines of the flying whale, filled with 150,000 cubic metres of hydrogen. Bruno felt a wave of something approaching panic wash over him as he considered the extreme precariousness of it all, this great balloon full of flammable gas, its structure at once so solid-looking and so fragile, and the madness of the men who lived inside the monster's stomach, manipulating its innards.

Eckener noticed the disquiet on Bruno's face. With a wicked smile, the commander pointed to a ladder leading to the top of the gigantic balloon. 'Perhaps you would like to climb up to the observation post on top of the hull, to make sure no stowaway is clinging to the outside of the ship?' he asked, before immediately apologizing for the joke.

It was a long journey along the axial gangway until they reached the ladder which led down to the base of the airship and the crew's lodgings. After descending the ladder, they came out on another gangway, which ran along the bottom of the hull. Beds hung on either side of the walkway, like sailors' hammocks in caravels of old, Bruno thought. There was also a tiny communal space with a few tables and chairs, beyond which the gangway continued towards the back of the hull, leading to the fuel tanks, cargo area and the crew's toilets.

Forty people, thought Bruno, cramming themselves into that misshapen balloon, crossing the ocean twenty times a year. It occurred to him just how horribly suicidal were those missions of the Great War, when men were ordered to fly in flammable bags of gas to drop bombs on London, awaiting the inevitable moment when some enemy bullet perforated the hull, and they would have to choose between being engulfed by a sea of flames or leaping out into the void. An army of Icaruses.

What a terrible sight they must have been from the ground. The harpy howl of the air-raid sirens, the night skies, raked by cannons of light, invaded by schools of these leviathans of the air coming to rain down death, until they were vanquished and burst into flames in the heavens, like visions of the divine.

How frightful, and at the same time, how wonderful. He would give anything to have seen it with his own eyes.

'I think it's best we turn back,' Bruno suggested, in a cold sweat.

'Oh, I thought you wanted to interrogate the crew? Come, let me show you, there's a secondary command deck in the airship's tail, which—'

'Let's return to the gondola, commander,' Bruno repeated, firmly.

'Of course, Herr Brückner, as you wish.'

They climbed back up to the axial gangway, which Bruno traversed with quick, nervous steps, before climbing back down the ladder to the navigation room, the commander following behind.

Back in the reassuring surroundings of the gondola, Bruno went to the galley, where he found Kubis telling an indignant chef and his assistant that they must not serve tapioca soup until further notice; the three of them were squeezed between the electric stove, the cupboard of heavy porcelain crockery and the immense Victoria Arduino espresso machine.

'Chief Steward Kubis,' Bruno interrupted, 'can you ask Mr Hay to meet me in the interview cabin in five minutes? Tell him... Tell him I need his professional opinion on an artistic matter.'

'Would you like an *apéritif* to whet your appetites?'

'Now that you mention it, yes. A whisky and soda for me... and whatever each of the passengers asks for when they're called too. At this stage in the journey, you must know their orders by heart.'

'Certainly.' Chief Steward Kubis nodded and left the galley.

Six

A SHORT while after, Mr William Hay appeared at the door to the interview cabin.

From what Chief Steward Kubis had told them, William Hay's father had made a large fortune importing coffee from Brazil to England before the war. This had allowed his son to abandon his studies at university and spend the last few years living a life of excessive liberality in the cabarets of the Weimar Republic, feeding his claims to be living as a writer, poet, literary critic or some other profession of uncertain prestige and scarce remuneration. William Hay, or Willy, as he insisted on being called, was never short of money, and consequently not used to being intimidated by police investigations.

He looked surprised by the scene he encountered: Bruno Brückner was sitting on the sofa, by the window, his hand resting on the bedside table, while the commander was standing by the door.

'It's a bit crowded in here, isn't it?' the Englishman said.

'Make yourself comfortable, Mr Hay.' Bruno gestured towards the sofa.

'Please, call me Willy.' Mr Hay sat down. 'How can I be of use to you, gentlemen?'

'Does the name Jonas Kurtzberg mean anything to you?' Bruno asked, showing him the deceased's passport, with the photograph of the man previously known as Otto Klein. 'Jonas Shmuel Kurtzberg, to be more precise.'

William Hay looked shocked when he heard the name. Then he frowned and darted a confused glance from Bruno to the commander, as he took in the scene. Next, he saw the papers on the table and must have recognized the covers of *Die Insel* and *Der Eigene*, because his expression changed entirely, becoming one of perfect relaxation.

A knock came at the door: it was Chief Steward Kubis, bringing a whisky and soda for Bruno and a Martini for Mr Hay. He served the drinks and left.

'Ah!' Mr Hay took a sip of his cocktail, leant back in his seat and crossed his legs, his face forming into a cunning, Cheshire cat smile. 'Yes, I knew I recognized the name from somewhere. I wasn't wrong, from what I can see.'

'So you knew him?'

'Only by sight, across a smoky cabaret or two, you know how these things go… But I'm very familiar with his *work*.' He gestured at the magazine with his glass. 'You can see for yourself. He's credited with many of the photos in these magazines. They're good. His compositions are more modern than those of Baron von Gloeden. The classical spirit *inspires* the composition but doesn't turn it into a simulation of the past. And yet, you never see a good prick in Kurtzberg's photos, the phallus is always suggested, symbolic. You do in von Gloeden's. In his pictures, the pricks come *au naturel*. Some say it's more erotic when something is merely suggested, not shown. But in my opinion, they're distinct aesthetics. One could accuse von Gloeden of having been very traditional, but a beautiful Italian cock, captured at ease, as if the model were a living sculpture, certainly had its value.'

Commander Eckener had turned red with embarrassment.

'"Had"?' Bruno asked, in a jovial tone. 'It doesn't any more?'

'Von Gloeden died three years ago,' Willy Hay explained. 'And Mussolini ordered all his work to be confiscated and destroyed. Perhaps the odd piece has fallen into the hands of a collector and been saved.'

'Naturally. It's for them, I imagine, that the majority of these photos are taken, isn't it?' Bruno said, pointing at the scattered photos. 'The *hands* of collectors. Do you believe that's why Jonas Kurtzberg was travelling incognito?'

'"Was travelling?" He's not travelling any more?' It was Willy Hay's turn to be jovial. 'Where is he? It's not as if there are many places to go inside this thing.'

'Jonas Kurtzberg was murdered at dawn, *mein Herr*,' the commander said.

Willy paused.

'Murdered... How?'

'A lethal dose of cyanide,' Bruno explained.

'Cyanide? My goodness.' Willy digested this information. 'But then it was a suicide, clearly.'

'What makes you think that?'

'It seems to me the most obvious conclusion. I've heard that's what spies did in the war: they swallowed capsules of cyanide to avoid being taken prisoner.'

'Do you believe Jonas Kurtzberg was a spy, then? For whom?'

'Well... the Bolsheviks, who else? I don't mean a real spy, perhaps just an agent in Moscow's service. Or merely a closeted communist, fleeing the purges. At the end of the day, he was linked to the Communist Party of Germany. That is, before you Nazis banned it on your very first day in government. And he was a Jew, as well. Isn't it just like the baroness said last night? Or was it the doctor? That every Jew is a Bolshevik?'

'You seemed to agree with the ideas expressed by Dr Voegler and the baroness at dinner last night, Mr Hay,' Bruno said. 'Now, your tone seems to me to be a little, how shall I put it... critical? Where do your political sympathies lie?'

'Oh, I was just being polite with them. I was clearly in a minority on that table and I wasn't going to ruin a pleasant evening.'

'A minority? Which one?' Bruno opted to approach head on. 'Are you a communist, Mr Hay?'

'No!' Willy said firmly, even irritably. 'But since you ask, I do consider myself a supporter of the labour movement. I believe in socialism and democracy. In my opinion, what Stalin did was corrupt the ideals of communism, imposing his dogmatic interpretation of Marxist theories, and, most of all, his personality cult.' He took another sip of his Martini. 'In any case, criticisms aside, it's undeniable that the free market inevitably corrupts democracy. You heard what the baroness said last night. None of those men put money into Hitler's hand with thoughts of maintaining democracy. And people such as yourself, Herr Brückner, are doubtless untroubled by that fact. Commander Eckener, who is a good man, may not be. If you had put yourself forward, commander, and I have heard you almost did, I would have voted for you. Were I German, of course.'

'Which brings me to the question,' Bruno said. 'What was a man with so much disdain for German values doing in Germany?'

'German values?' Willy laughed. 'What, Nazi values?'

'Nazi values are *not* German values,' Commander Eckener protested, to which Willy smiled, closing his eyes and raising his Martini glass as if making a toast.

He took a final sip and handed the glass to Bruno, who put it on the table.

'At least not when I first went there,' Willy said, finishing the commander's sentence. 'I went to Germany to escape from people like you on my own little island. Moralists. What was England at the time? A country that found it acceptable to censor Joyce's work! Where any old magistrate felt they had the right to walk into the Warren gallery and remove D.H. Lawrence's paintings, claiming they were indecent! Why, when censorship reaches the arts, any free-spirited young person comes to the same conclusion: time to leave. The Americans fled the repression of Prohibition by going to drink in Paris. In England, we had a different kind of repression, so we went to Berlin. Ah, the cabarets! The parties in El Dorado. The nudist beaches! Not to mention Hamburg!

Nights in Sankt Pauli... The freedom of going to a magazine stand and buying the latest edition of *Die Insel*... But then you Nazis started to gain power. At first, I didn't take it very seriously, it seemed like nothing more than a gang of braggarts organizing in their shooting clubs, a handful of nationalist professors brainwashing a few students with messianic speeches here and there. And the generals, of course, giving out medals like sweets. All those officials swanning about the streets with their gongs—Berlin was beginning to look like one big army barracks.'

Willy stayed silent for a moment. When he spoke again, he turned to Commander Eckener.

'And then the threats began, the persecutions, the beatings. And now anyone worth knowing is leaving. Germany's over, essentially: time to leave. So I thought I'd get acquainted with Brazil, which is ultimately where our money comes from. My father, as I imagine you know, is one of the major coffee importers in England.'

'Ah, yes. Brazil.' Bruno showed him the copy of *Die Insel*. 'Does this young man on the cover look familiar to you?'

'No. Should he?'

'The photo credit says that it was sent by a reader from Rio de Janeiro,' Bruno explained. 'I don't know, it may be just a coincidence, or perhaps it is someone Jonas

Kurtzberg was going to meet in Rio. Someone he might have met in Berlin? In a smoky cabaret?'

'Unlikely,' Willy said. 'Look here, *Die Insel* has subscribers worldwide, it's quite a popular magazine, unlike its rival, which is very elitist. Or, rather, was. Your lot shut both down earlier this year.'

'Have you ever written for either of them?' Bruno asked.

'Why are you asking a question to which you already know the answer?' Willy smiled. 'Yes, I used to write reviews for *Der Eigene*, the rival magazine.'

'What was the nature of this… rivalry?' Commander Eckener asked.

'Nothing that would justify a murder, if that's what you're insinuating.'

'I'm not insinuating anything, Mr Hay, merely—'

'As I said, please call me Willy. Mr Hay is my father,' he said with a smile. 'Radszuweit, the editor of *Die Insel*, is a highly pragmatic type, irremediably optimistic, I fear. And with good business sense. He believes that reading contributes to the creation of a sense of community, and that the right balance between entertainment and politics can result in practical action. His publications are more accessible, he isn't afraid of resorting to a certain *risqué* eroticism and of showing the reader that he is not alone in the world, that homosexual love isn't restricted to Ancient

Greece and classical paintings and half a dozen erudite works. And he wanted to appeal to as wide an audience as possible, not just homosexual men. He used to publish an excellent magazine for lesbians as well: *Die Freundin*. And *Das dritte Geschlecht*, for transvestites. And he promoted lavish parties for homosexuals and transvestites, *Puppenbälle*, which... Well, *those* were parties, all right.'

'And what was the nature of his rivalry with *Der Eigene*?'

Willy sighed, pulling a face that showed he considered the question tedious.

'Adolf Brand, the editor of *Der Eigene*, is an idealist. And he had serious literary ambitions for his magazine. He was always complaining that homosexuals are more interested in partying in cabarets than in literature. Brand believes in egoist anarchism and criticizes Radszuweit's "lack of idealism", while Radszuweit in turn criticizes Brand's "lack of pragmatism". Aside from that, Brand's vision for homosexual culture is somewhat... elitist, strictly masculine, excessively Greek, so to speak. That is, he cares little about lesbians, transvestites or even effeminate men. He's bisexual, by the way. I found out he married a woman. Which according to Radszuweit makes him just another heterosexual wanting to profit from homosexuals.'

Bruno looked at Commander Eckener.

The commander nodded. Bruno showed the loose photograph to Willy.

'Does this young man look familiar?'

'No. Should he?' He turned over the photograph and saw the name written on the reverse. 'Ah, Fridolin! Yes, of course, that makes sense. He possesses the kind of beauty that an aesthete like Kurtzberg would appreciate. He was always appearing in the society columns next to his aunt, but I can't have seen him in person more than once or twice.'

'Across a smoky cabaret?' Bruno scoffed.

'Across a smoky cabaret,' Willy confirmed. 'I heard some stories… they involved sailors and a ship from Brest. He has been the cause of several broken hearts and at least one cut throat. I don't know the details. Obviously, it was all hushed up and the boy was sent abroad. At the end of the day, his uncle is van Hattem, one of your party's greatest funders. Ah! If the baroness only knew she was sitting across the table from Jonas Kurtzberg! Face to face with one of the "degenerates" she probably believes corrupted her little angel…'

'You don't think that could have been the case?'

'Why of course not! It wasn't Kurtzberg who led Fridolin down the 'wrong track', no more than the dancers at El Dorado, the *Strichjungen* of Sankt Pauli or half the entire French navy, if what I've heard is true.'

'No, I was referring to the baroness,' Bruno said, irritated. 'Could she have realized who Kurtzberg was and taken revenge on the man she deemed responsible for perverting her nephew?'

'Perhaps. Poisoning is a feminine act, isn't it? I always remember Lucrezia Borgia. I don't know where she would have got the cyanide. Although we did have tapioca soup at dinner last night, of course.'

'What's that got to do with it?' Commander Eckener demanded.

'What, you didn't know?' Willy said. 'Tapioca is made from cassava. Which is the plant with the highest concentration of cyanide.'

Bruno and the commander glanced at one another. Eckener went pale.

'I didn't know that,' the commander said.

Willy finished his Martini and asked if they had any more questions. They both said no, asking only that he be discreet and not mention anything to the other passengers before they had reached a conclusion.

Seven

BARONESS Fridegunde van Hattem came through the door animated and smiling, as if someone had just told her a joke. To justify calling her to the cabin they had said there had been a problem with her baggage and that the commander needed to speak with her in private.

'Oh! *Der Polizist und der Kommandant!*' she sighed. 'Well, I saw my jewels not long ago, just before going to the dining room, so it's not possible that someone could have—' The door opened and Kubis appeared with a gin and tonic on his tray. 'Oh, no thank you! It's like that song, "*Mama don't want no gin because it would make her sin*". I had my fair share last night!'

'Of gin or of sin?' Bruno jested, smiling.

'Oh, Herr Brückner, you are wicked!' she laughed. 'So then, what is it? As I said, I only recently checked my jewels in my cabin. Don't tell me someone has stolen them already! So soon? Although, who knows, with these Brazilians on board? They're all half-breeds, and you can't trust—'

'It's nothing to do with that, baroness,' Bruno said. 'I'm afraid it's something more serious. Tell me, do you have children?'

'No, no. But I have a nephew, Fridolin. *Mein Gott!* Has something happened to him? Did you receive a message?'

'No, not at all. But I would like to clarify some matters first. Tell me about your nephew.'

'I don't understand. What has he got to do with this?'

'A crime has occurred on board,' Bruno explained. 'And your nephew's name appeared on some documents found with the victim. I'd like to…'

'Victim?' The baroness started. 'What kind of crime are we talking about?'

'If you don't mind, baroness, I'll ask the questions,' Bruno said, gently but firmly, and smiled.

The baroness bristled. She was not used to receiving orders, only to giving them, and she never hesitated to remind anyone who got in her way of their inferior social status.

'Please watch your tone,' she said. 'I think I have the right to know what this is about, after all.'

'A man was murdered on board, baroness. He was travelling with a fake passport and your nephew's name was among his documents. We're trying to establish who exactly he was, and we believe you can help us with that. Which is why we need you to talk about your nephew.'

'Oh, I see.' She seemed more at ease. 'Now, please call Chief Steward Kubis back. I'll take that gin and tonic now.'

The commander left the cabin for a moment. Bruno and the baroness exchanged cordial smiles.

'I think we can—' Bruno started.

'Let's wait for my gin and tonic,' the baroness interrupted.

The commander returned with the drink. The baroness thanked him, took a sip and said:

'Fridolin's father was my brother, a cavalry officer who died in the Somme offensive in 1916. His mother died of tuberculosis soon after. Fridolin was only six at the time and has lived with us since then. He's like a son to us. Such a sweet boy, he's never given us any trouble. Yes, he's twenty-four now, but I still call him a boy, because he'll always be my boy. Almost an angel! He's so intelligent, polite and helpful. He's very religious too. He always accompanies me to mass! He's nothing like these young men today, who only want to know about parties, gin and jazz.'

'Do you disapprove of gin and jazz?'

'Gin, if taken in moderation, is not a problem. But jazz is totally improper. The infusion of black blood into German culture must not be encouraged. As you know, black music is always degenerate. Monkeys playing trumpets. You'll see for yourself when we disembark in Rio de Janeiro. They too have their own problem with this, with black music.'

'But wasn't that song you were humming just a moment ago, when you were first offered a gin and tonic, a jazz number?'

'Ah, but *I*, my dear, am discerning. The problem is with the masses.'

'Anyway, baroness, I don't know if the victim drank gin or listened to jazz, but the fact is, your nephew's name was written on one of his documents, and we ventured that you might know him. His name was Jonas Kurtzberg.'

'No, I've never heard of him. But there's no way I could know *all* of Fridolin's friends. He's a *very* popular lad, you see.'

'I can imagine.'

'Who is this Kurtzberg, anyway?'

'You met him last night, but under another name. He introduced himself as Otto Klein.'

She looked surprised.

'Ah! Then Mr Hay was right? He really was a Jew? Incidentally, where is he now?'

'Baroness, Herr Kurtzberg was murdered today at dawn.'

'Oh...'

She stayed silent for some time, taking in the information. Then she downed her gin and tonic in a single gulp.

'And how did he die? What was he doing here anyway?'

'From what we have discovered from looking at his hand baggage, he was working as a photographer for some magazines. And he was poisoned with cyanide.'

'*Mein Gott!* A terrible poison,' the baroness said, adding casually, 'but very efficient, you know? When used in the correct dose there is sufficient time for the poisoner to get away before the victim dies. Hours, sometimes. And it's very easy to find. Bitter almonds or apricot stones are great sources of cyanide. I have read that the symptoms can include dizziness, vomiting, flushing, drowsiness, accelerated pulse and unconsciousness...'

'You've done considerable reading on this topic, it would appear?' Bruno asked. 'You seem to know a lot about how cyanide works.'

'I know what you're thinking, don't you go getting any ideas!' she laughed, making a gesture in the air as if shooing away a fly. 'I've been fascinated by the story of Lucrezia Borgia ever since I watched Donizetti's opera.

The Borgias preferred arsenic, which was frequently used as a tonic in Grandma's time. Since then, I've been very interested in how poisons work. But... the poor man! What a horrible death. Who could have killed him?'

'We don't know yet. That's why we called you here. The late Herr Klein, or Kurtzberg, was carrying some publications with him that indicate his connections with the movement for homosexual rights. But for some reason the English gentleman, Mr Hay, is inclined to believe that Kurtzberg was an undercover communist agent.'

'Ah, yes... I understand.' Her expression changed completely, her smile turning into an expression of cold indifference. 'Well then, the son of a bitch got what he deserved,' she hissed through gritted teeth.

Bruno raised an eyebrow in surprise.

'Come on, don't look at me like that.' The baroness raised her chin in defiance. 'The Bolsheviks deserve no less than what they do to people like us. Remember what they did to the Tsar! Dr Voegler was right last night when he said that the communists are our greatest threat. Wanting to put everyone on the same level. I mean, come on. Can you imagine a more *impractical* vision of the world? After all, if everyone was equal, what would be the point in having a lot of money? The more things one has, the more one desires, and expectations continue to change and increase day by day, only it's not that simple. The great thing is to possess exclusive items, to which only we have access. If everyone has access to those pleasures, they lose their attraction.'

Bruno looked at the magazines on the table next to him and hesitated over whether to show them to the baroness.

'To return to the matter in question, baroness: the only people who had any contact with the victim were those who dined with Jonas Kurtzberg last night,' Bruno pointed out. 'He retired rather early, seemingly in a hurry, you'll recall, just after Mr Hay had provoked him with insinuations regarding his Judaean origin. Then, this morning, he was found dead in the men's lavatory.'

'Oh! So that's why the men were using our one. He must have been in there all night.'

'That's the crux of it. A little after four in the morning, after the airmail packages had been thrown out in Salvador, Mr Hay says he heard footsteps in the corridor more than once, but wasn't sure of the time. Did you hear anything, baroness?'

'Ah, no, I heard nothing. I must confess I slept like Snow White.'

'Don't you mean Sleeping Beauty?'

'Come, Snow White also fell into a slumber, didn't she?'

'Yes, true,' Bruno agreed. 'But only after being poisoned…'

'Well, Herr Brückner, if you will allow me, it's lunchtime and I'm rather peckish. I have no idea why this degenerate communist Jew had my Fridolin's name among his things. Perhaps he was trying to use it against me, to blackmail or embarrass me? After the things those horrible unions did in my Helmut's factory, nothing would surprise me! It must be the Bolshevik Jew's impulse towards destruction. If that's the case, it makes sense that he would have killed himself with a cyanide capsule.'

'I didn't say anything about cyanide capsules.'

'You didn't? Well, that's how they do it in spy stories, isn't it? I saw a film like that. Or was it a book? In any case, I'm happy this so-and-so is dead. I shall propose a toast to Mr Hay for having helped to unmask him last night.'

'Oh no,' the commander intervened. 'Please, don't say anything to anyone until we have concluded our investigation. The other passengers must not know, baroness.'

'Of course, naturally, what am I thinking? We can't let this communist riffraff ruin the last hours of this adorable trip of ours.'

She moved to get up but Bruno raised his hand.

'One more question, baroness.'

'Yes?'

'Your nephew. The paper on which his name was written... is a photograph. Nothing obscene, I assure you. Just a photograph that looks like it was taken on some beach on the Baltic. If you could take a look and confirm that—'

'Thank you, I won't be looking at anything.' She stood up.

'Baroness, we just need you to confirm that—'

'Herr Brückner, if my nephew's name is mentioned in any way in association with that parasitic worm, my family will use every reasonable means to punish whoever is responsible for that insult. I don't like to put it in such terms, but people like you should know their place. You are merely a member of the *Kriminalpolizei*, nothing more. My husband is close to the *Reichsführer* himself, Himmler.'

She turned to Eckener.

'Would you please open the door, commander?'

He obeyed. The baroness trotted out of the cabin without another word.

Commander Eckener pulled his watch out of his pocket and told Bruno he needed to go to the *Steuerraum* to see how things were with Knut, but that he would be back soon.

'Shall I collect Dr Voegler on my way back?' the commander asked. 'They're about to serve lunch.'

'Oh, I'd hate to have to interrupt Dr Voegler's meal...' Bruno said. And then, assuming the bureaucratic, indifferent tone of voice that would become characteristic of his party's officials, he added:

'Tell him it's a medical emergency. And ask him to bring his suitcase.'

Eight

Dr Voegler entered the cabin with a look of concern on his face, Commander Eckener following close behind him. The doctor was surprised to see Bruno sitting on the sofa, casually leafing through *Die Insel*.

'Herr Brückner! What's happened? Are you all right?'

'Please, Dr Voegler, sit.' Bruno tossed the magazine onto the bedside table and looked at the doctor. 'I felt slightly dizzy and nauseous, so I asked the commander to call you.'

'Perhaps something at breakfast didn't agree with you?'

'I don't think so. I didn't eat anything that I am not accustomed to. However, last night, after that tapioca soup… I was worried, because I've heard cassava contains high levels of cyanide.'

'Oh, yes, there is a specific kind of cassava that is very rich in hydrogen cyanide, but only if it's undercooked or eaten raw. And it's unlikely we would have been supplied with that variety in Recife. Besides, other passengers would also have been affected if you were.'

The door opened. Chief Steward Kubis appeared, carrying a glass of sparkling water for Dr Voegler, then left immediately.

'I've nothing to worry about, then?' Bruno asked.

'Not at all. You seem to me to be in perfect health.' Dr Voegler looked at the commander and then back at Bruno. 'Is there something else?'

'Unfortunately, doctor, yes there is,' Bruno said, handing him the magazines.

'*Ach!* What is this? Where did they come from?'

'We found them in the cabin of a fellow passenger. We don't know his relationship to these magazines, but I would like you, sir, to tell me more about the kind of person that might be interested in this sort of publication. Your professional opinion on the matter. I remember that last night you said something about your involvement with a certain Dr Hirschfeld's Institut für Sexualwissenschaft in Berlin, about which I know nothing.'

'"Involvement", no! Nothing of the sort! My only involvement, if you can call it that, was to get rid of that cesspit of degeneracy,' Dr Voegler said, irritated. 'Hirschfeld… that man is a danger to the Germanic nation, a threat to the purification of the Aryan race, the *Volk*.'

He explained that Magnus Hirschfeld was a Jewish doctor who had founded an 'Institute for Sexual Research' in Berlin. His objective was clear: to reverse paragraph 175 of the German Penal Code, which criminalized sexual relations between men. To that end, he had sponsored scientific studies and publications and even produced a film to be shown in cinemas, *Anders als die Andern* (Different from the Others), as well as organizing an open letter which was signed by famous figures such as Einstein, Stefan Zweig and Rilke, among others.

'That man is such a degenerate that he even supervised an operation to *change a man's sex*! Can you imagine such a thing?' Dr Voegler said, indignant. 'He said that the persecution of homosexuals was as barbarous as the medieval witch hunts and that France's Napoleonic Code was an example to be followed since, wherever it was introduced, police persecution of homosexuals stopped. Well! Tell me, isn't this sort of Francophilia proof in itself that giving rights to degenerates is the least Germanic thing one could do?'

'I confess I have never given it much thought,' Bruno said. 'As a police officer, I prefer to spend my time attending to other affairs rather than going after such people. However, it is my job, and there seems to be no end to them. I suppose you're right.'

'I understand your weariness. *Reichsführer* Himmler estimates that there are close to two million homosexuals in Germany, which is nearly ten per cent of the country's men. If that is true, then our nation will sooner or later be destroyed by this plague. If these men are no longer capable of maintaining relationships with women, that will upset the balance between the sexes, which will be our ruin. We will become an *effeminate* nation. And having so few children will do nothing to advance our race's superiority. We must be very clear on this matter: if we continue to bear this burden it will be the end of Germany and the Germanic world. Homosexuals *must* be eliminated.'

'*Mein Gott*, doctor,' Bruno said. 'I was thinking in terms of expulsion, not elimination. Some of those men have wives or children, and even if they don't, we must assume they have fathers and mothers. Would there not be protests, uproar, even?'

'Now, Herr Brückner, I'm sure we agree on this... Who would be capable of loving a homosexual son?' He took a sip of his water. 'Let's not be hypocrites. Would you? Personally, I'd prefer my son die in some "accident" than to see him cavorting in the arms of a moustachioed man. But, of course, there's no risk of this because my children were well brought up, they did not experience the kinds of environments which have, lamentably, been seen in recent years, the cabarets flooded with cheap drink and negro music.'

He handed the magazines back to Bruno, who dropped them onto the table.

'Perhaps you are better informed than I am,' Bruno said. 'Far be it from me to wish to spread rumours on the matter, but it's curious that *Reichsführer* Himmler should have said all that regarding degenerates'—Bruno lowered his voice—'since I have heard from a reliable source that *Stabschef* Röhm and several members of his *Sturmtruppen* were loyal clients at the El Dorado nightclub, a well-known Berlin cabaret, which—'

'Yes, I remember a scandal around the time of the elections,' Dr Voegler mumbled. 'At the time, I considered it mere counterpropaganda. But Himmler knows what he's saying and doing. If Röhm really is a homosexual... well, then the party will take care of it. "*Deutschland über alles*," as our anthem says. Now, it's your turn to tell me something: who is the degenerate that brought these magazines on board?'

'You won't believe it: our nervous tablemate from last night, Herr Otto Klein.'

'You don't say! I knew there was something wrong with him.'

'There's more: that wasn't even his real name. He was using a fake passport. His real name was Jonas Shmuel Kurtzberg.'

'So, he is a Jew!' Dr Voegler exclaimed. 'Mr Hay was right, after all. But I didn't see this Kurtzberg at breakfast today. Where is he?'

'Dead,' said Commander Eckener, in a dry, irritable voice.

Dr Voegler seemed shocked. He looked at Bruno as if in search of answers, and when he saw the stern expression on his face, he sighed.

'Ah, I see. Now your questions about cyanide make sense. Was he poisoned, is that it? But there's no way… It can't have been the tapioca soup, that much is certain.'

'May I see your briefcase, doctor?'

'Of course,' he said warily, handing the case to Bruno. 'But I guarantee you'll not find anything out of the ordinary in there. I certainly do not carry any cyanide with me.'

Bruno opened his briefcase and examined the instruments and medications inside it. Then he took out a vial of tonic and read the label: 'Fowler's solution'. It contained a percentage of potassium arsenate, or arsenic.

'All the rage in Grandma's day,' Bruno muttered.

'Pardon?'

Bruno waved his hand dismissively. It would have taken an enormous dose of the tonic to kill, and the bottle was full. Then he found another vial, and his face lit up.

He took it out of the briefcase and held it up between his thumb and index finger, so that both the doctor and the commander could see. This vial was not full. Some of the liquid was missing.

'Hydrochloric acid,' Dr Voegler said, bristling. 'I use it to test purity. What's wrong with that?'

'Oh, I forgot to tell you, doctor. Jonas Kurtzberg was a photographer. And among his belongings was a vial containing Prussian blue.'

Dr Voegler turned pale.

'But… but… why… how could I have known that?'

'You couldn't have,' Bruno reassured him. 'I'm not assuming you did. It's just a coincidence. The victim, a homosexual Jew, was poisoned with cyanide. We know that Prussian blue, when combined with hydrochloric acid, produces a gas cloud that can be fatal. I imagine someone must have entered Kurtzberg's cabin at dawn and mixed the hydrochloric acid with a little Prussian blue. That would have had the effect of transforming the cabin into a veritable gas chamber, like the ones the Americans use to execute their criminals.'

It was Dr Voegler's turn, having drained his glass of water, to lean back in his seat and smile confidently.

'Highly imaginative, Herr Brückner,' the doctor said. 'But you're wrong on two counts: I didn't know the fellow's identity until this very moment, and even now that I do, I don't see what reason I could have to waste my time murdering him in such a complex way, on board an airship which, I should remind you, is the pride of Germany, making a scandal highly likely. Not that he didn't deserve to die, incidentally. A degenerate like Hirschfeld from a subhuman race will not be missed. But even had I known who he was and had a great desire to murder him, I would need to have known beforehand that he was carrying a vial of Prussian blue in his hand baggage and have entered his cabin without being seen, and done all of this without waking the presumed victim. Wouldn't it have been easier just to knock him on the head?'

'I agree, and it is far from my intention to accuse you, doctor,' Bruno said. 'But, as you yourself mentioned, you woke at dawn. Mr Hay heard someone walking down the corridor, and you yourself admitted that on at least one of those occasions it was you going to the washroom. And it's important to add that Jonas Kurtzberg was not found dead in his cabin but in the WC next to the washroom.'

'The door of which remained locked until midmorning. I would have needed a master key to lock it from the outside, which, I should remind you, *only Chief Steward Kubis possesses*. And if I locked it from the inside, how did I get out again? Perhaps I evaporated on one side of the door and reformed on the other, like Count Dracula? Or do you think it possible that I could have entered the Jew's cabin, produced a highly toxic gas, which somehow did not affect me, and still had time to leave the victim's cabin and return to my own, while the fellow woke up, ran to the WC, locked the door and dropped dead?'

'I agree, it's rather improbable,' Bruno said. 'But not impossible. As I once read somewhere, "when you have excluded the impossible, whatever remains, however improbable, must be the truth". And the fact remains: the only people the victim interacted with on the airship were those who dined with him last night.'

'Including Kubis, who served us,' Dr Voegler reminded him. 'And he has the master key.'

'Chief Steward Kubis's integrity is above suspicion!' Commander Eckener protested.

'I'm not trying to insinuate anything, commander,' the doctor said. 'But have you considered a hypothesis of suicide? I remember reading about a case in the papers, an English man who, having been sentenced for fraud, ingested cyanide during the trial. Perhaps that's what the Jew did, who knows.'

'Strange, both Mr Hay and Baroness van Hattem suggested that hypothesis,' Bruno observed. 'Mr Hay even believed that the chap was some sort of undercover communist.'

'Wait a minute… This fellow was a Jew, a homosexual and, as if that wasn't enough, a communist too?' Dr Voegler laughed. 'Do we really need to be making such a fuss about this?'

'The Brazilian police will want to know what happened,' the commander pointed out.

'Well, that's true,' Dr Voegler agreed. 'In that case, perhaps you should check those enormous rings on the baroness's hands. Or ask what would lead an Englishman on board a German airship to be so certain that another passenger is a spy. After all, if you recall, the first person to call Otto Klein's identity into question was our dear Mr Hay.'

Bruno nodded slowly in agreement.

'Consider the possibility of death by suicide, Herr Brückner. If it's of any use, I can provide a death certificate to confirm it.'

'Thank you, *Herr Doktor*, I'll take your kind offer into consideration. In any case, thank you for this information. I'm sorry if I put you on the spot, but it was necessary to explore all the possibilities.'

'Not at all, *mein Herr*. I understand that it's your duty.'

Bruno got up from the sofa, returned the briefcase to Dr Voegler and the two men shook hands. After the doctor had left, the commander asked:

'So, have you managed to come to any conclusions?'

'I need to reflect on the matter. What time is it? And where exactly are we now?'

'It's almost one in the afternoon. In an hour's time we shall be approaching the city of Vitória.'

'Hmm.' Bruno stroked his chin pensively. 'What time are we scheduled to arrive in Rio de Janeiro?'

'As long as there are no headwinds, we're forecast to reach Rio de Janeiro between midnight and one in the morning. Given the late hour, we will fly over Guanabara Bay for a few hours and not disembark until the morning, at around six.'

'Then that's how much time I have to reach a conclusion,' Bruno announced. 'Until then, I will keep a close eye on our suspects to see if I notice anything else.'

'Perfect.' The commander went to open the cabin door, but hesitated. 'One last thing, Herr Brückner. Do you have any reason to suspect Chief Steward Kubis?'

'To be frank with you, commander, no, none. Why? Do you?'

'No, not in the slightest. He's been with us for decades, and I would hate to imagine he has any involvement in this.'

Having said this, he opened the door and they both went out.

Nine

Lunch was delicious. The starter of tomato soup was followed by roasted pork chops with red cabbage, pea puree and cucumber salad. For dessert, lemon tart with custard.

Bruno Brückner lunched with a Brazilian couple who didn't speak a single word of German. Talking to them, he discovered that his meagre knowledge of Portuguese was sufficient for basic conversation but not enough to understand everything they were saying. And these Brazilians spoke very fast. And they talked and talked. After a certain point, Bruno did little more than smile and nod in polite agreement.

Baroness van Hattem, Dr Voegler and Mr Hay were all seated at separate tables. Chief Steward Kubis circulated among the diners with his customary affability, but from time to time glanced anxiously over at Bruno.

Captain Eckener showed his face and chatted briefly with the diners. His son, the helmsman Knut, appeared at the door, glanced briefly at Bruno and returned to the command deck.

After lunch, Bruno found Commander Eckener in the *Steuerraum* and explained that he wished to gather together the three main suspects, Chief Steward Kubis and the commander, so that he could present his conclusions to their faces. But he didn't see where he could discreetly bring together six people within the confines of the *Graf Zeppelin*.

'Yes, there's really only one place we can use,' Commander Eckener said. 'Right here.'

Bruno looked around him: the *Steuerraum* was spacious enough for six or seven people to stand inside it. The only problem was the two window-like openings into the navigation room.

'I can limit the navigation team to the minimum necessary,' the commander said.

'Is anyone in the crew affiliated with the Nazi Party?'

'Captain Lehmann and navigators Pruss and Wittemann are Nazis.'

'Let it be them, then,' Bruno said.

Eckener raised a suspicious eyebrow.

'I hope you don't mind my asking, but why?'

'*Führerprinzip*, commander. The principle of

leadership set out by Hitler,' Bruno said. '"The leader is always right", his word is law. And the conclusions I have reached, commander, will require a solution that is... drastic and unprecedented. It will appear cruel at first, but the true Nazis will recognize its legitimacy and obey intuitively.'

Commander Eckener frowned.

'They are loyal to me.'

'And they will continue to be so, commander. Even you will agree that the conclusion to this situation is inevitable.' Bruno looked around him, beyond the glass windows of the cabin, towards the sky and the clouds under the late afternoon sun. 'Where are we now?'

'We're approaching Cape São Tomé,' the commander said.

'It's a lovely day.'

'Yes. We'll have a beautiful sunset.'

As the end of the afternoon approached and he went from table to table serving coffee, biscuits and drinks, Chief Steward Kubis discreetly informed the three passengers that their presence would soon be required on the command deck, so that they could receive the explanations they were owed after that morning's conversations with Herr Brückner and the commander.

It was six in the evening when the chief steward knocked on the door of Bruno Brückner's cabin. He had spent the afternoon dozing on the sofa and was at that moment reading peacefully.

'They're all waiting for you, Herr Brückner.'

Bruno closed the book and accompanied Chief Steward Kubis along the corridor and across the dining room to the prow. When he entered the navigation room, adjacent to the command deck, the door was locked behind him.

In the navigation room were Captain Ernst Lehmann and navigators Max Pruss and Anton Wittemann. Two windows in the dividing wall communicated with the command deck. There, in front of the great glass window, with the clouds hanging above and the Brazilian coast spread out below, all bathed in the light of the orange sunset, the little group was gathered: Baroness Fridegunde van Hattem, Doctor Karl Kass Voegler, Mr William Hay and Chief steward Heinrich Kubis, with Commander Hugo Eckener at the helm.

Bruno took the floor.

'Ladies and gentlemen, I'll get straight to it. Here are the facts: a man was murdered on board the LZ 127 *Graf Zeppelin* at dawn today. The man, who boarded with a false passport in the name of Otto Klein, was actually a Jewish photographer called Jonas Kurtzberg. His body was found this morning in the men's lavatory, which was apparently locked from the inside. The cause of death was cyanide poisoning. It's hard to say *how* he was poisoned, but we can assume that the poison only began to take effect just before death, when the victim felt the urge to vomit and ran to the men's lavatory. This took place after four in the morning, when the mail bundles were thrown out in Salvador. Mr Hay claims to have heard footsteps marching up and down the corridor. Dr Voegler says that one of those times it was him going to the lavatory in the early morning. The baroness doesn't remember having heard anything, nor, honestly, do I. But here's what we have discovered about this Jew: first, he wasn't just any photographer, but rather a specialist in the kind of male nudes published in magazines aimed at homosexuals, whom Dr Voegler here detests with every fibre of his being. The good doctor has in his briefcase a vial of hydrochloric acid which could, in theory, be used to generate cyanide, if brought into contact with the Prussian blue dye we found among the victim's belongings.'

Dr Voegler puffed out his chest and made as if to protest, but Bruno raised a hand to silence him, continuing:

'Kurtzberg also had with him a photograph of Fridolin van Hattem, the baroness's nephew who—' Now it was the baroness's turn to grow indignant, but once again Bruno silenced her with a raised palm. 'Easy, baroness, there's nothing inherently compromising in the photograph, nor am I insinuating anything. All I was going to say was that this created an undeniable link to your name and opened up many possibilities in the investigation, including some kind of extortion, given the problems your husband's company has had with the unions in recent years. Ah, yes: it was also suggested that this chap might have been an undercover communist agent, who committed suicide upon sensing that his true identity was about to be revealed. Incidentally, according to Mr Hay this was very common behaviour for spies during the Great War. Given the circumstances, this was not a possibility I could ignore. Now, I too have read my quota of English novels, Mr Hay, and as entertaining as they are, I have not forgotten the anti-German sentiments in the books of H.G. Wells and Erskine Childers, not to mention John Buchan's *The 39 Steps*. In short, I've read enough to be suspicious of the intentions of any British subject journeying beyond their island. If you have any other evidence that Kurtzberg was a communist agent and want to reveal it to us now, be my guest...'

'As you said, it was just an inkling,' Mr Hay smiled. 'A *strong* inkling.'

'Evidently,' Bruno said. 'Finally, I must mention Chief Steward Kubis, who has carried out his role as maître d' of this luxury flying hotel in which we are all guests with the utmost refinement and competence. He also had contact with the victim, since he greeted him and served him all of his meals and drinks, although I can see no motive that would lead him to commit a crime of this kind while discharging his duties for a company he has served faithfully for more than twenty years. These are the facts.'

'Come on then, let's get this pantomime over and done with,' grunted Dr Voegler, grabbing the baroness's hand and raising it rather abruptly. 'Has anyone checked this woman's rings?'

'*I beg your pardon.* What are you thinking?' the baroness protested, pulling her arm away. 'What have my rings got to do with this?'

'Absolutely nothing. The same way Lucrezia Borgia's were completely innocent…'

'Please remain calm,' Bruno said. 'I've already reached a conclusion.'

Then he turned to Commander Eckener.

'Commander, Jonas Kurtzberg committed suicide.'

'What?' The commander was visibly shocked. 'Are you sure about that?'

'Not at all. But to carry out a full investigation, I would need a coroner's report, we'd have to interview all the passengers and crew, comb the entire airship for clues and inspect all the food supplied on board. That would be an enormous inconvenience to your passengers and delight newspapers across the world. After all, there's nothing people love to read about more than a scandal involving the rich and high-born. It would be bad publicity for the German government and bad publicity for your company, which, from what you yourself have told me, is already facing pressure from Minister Goebbels. And all for what? To seek justice for a homosexual and possibly communist Jew? Who was travelling under a false identity. Dr Voegler, don't you agree with me? Baroness? Mr Hay? Captain Lehmann, Herr Pruss, Herr Wittemann… Isn't it the goal of the Aryan cause to eradicate this cancer corrupting our society? Now, someone on this airship, someone *in this room*, got ahead of themselves and left this awkward situation for us all to deal with. It seems to me, therefore, that there is only one way out of this impasse.'

'And what would that be?' Commander Eckener asked.

'One you're not going to like much,' Bruno smiled. 'But it has the advantage of being very practical. However, it requires the agreement of all present. A pact, so to speak.'

They listened to his proposal.

Nodding in silence, they agreed with everything, even though some, including Eckener, his son Knut and Chief Steward Kubis, did so with visible distaste.

Outside, the sun was sinking into the western horizon, and the world below was filled with the beautiful, hazy light of dusk.

Dinner was served at nightfall.

The *Graf Zeppelin* was moving along the shoreline of the state of Rio de Janeiro, and from the windows the passengers could admire from above the lights of the city, with Guanabara Bay lit up by the fairy colours of the Urca Casino. At ten o'clock, a radio message announced that the Zeppelin would fly over Santos and São Paulo overnight, not landing in Rio de Janeiro until the morning.

At half past eleven, when all the passengers had already repaired to their cabins, Captain Lehmann and the navigators Pruss and Wittemann walked through the dining room and entered the victim's cabin. The body was rolled up in sheets and weights were tied to his feet. The case containing the magazines, photographs and passports was handed to Bruno, who would be responsible for burning them at the first opportunity after landing.

At midnight, while the passengers were sleeping, the Zeppelin's boarding gate was opened and a body was dropped into the waters of Guanabara Bay. It was not the first time and it would certainly not be the last.

The airship passed over São Paulo at dawn and began the last leg of its journey back to Rio de Janeiro. At four in the morning, Chief Steward Kubis went from door to door, rousing the passengers. The Brazilian capital was their final destination. From there the Zeppelin would return to Recife and then onwards to the United States. A queue formed as the passengers made use of the washroom and lavatories.

At six in the morning, the LZ 127 *Graf Zeppelin* lowered its altitude over the region of Campo dos Afonsos, west of Rio, near the School of Military Aviation. Commander Eckener had mentioned to Bruno that German engineers had already selected the area where a dedicated hangar would be built in the Brazilian capital for LZ airships, but the works still hadn't started.

First, the Zeppelin was boarded by men from customs, the maritime police and the port authority, for routine inspections. Next, the passengers started to disembark. On the runway, a driver from the Condor Syndicate approached Commander Eckener.

'Is there an Otto Klein on board? I've been told to find a Mr Otto Klein.' He pointed to the car. 'Connection for Buenos Aires.'

'No,' the commander said. 'His name was on the passenger list, but he did not board in Recife. We were not told of the reason. Perhaps he missed his flight or decided against it.'

The driver shrugged.

'How strange. All right, I'll let the office know.'

Bruno Brückner watched Mr William Hay walk past him and climb straight into a taxi without a word of goodbye or a backwards glance. Baroness Fridegunde van Hattem also took her leave with no more than a curt *auf Wiedersehen*. Only Dr Voegler made a point of saying goodbye. Before he got into the car that would take him to his connection for São Paulo, he called over to Bruno.

'I'd just like to say, Herr Brückner, that, given the circumstances, your solution to the problem was ideal. And rather elegant, too.'

'Thank you, *Herr Doktor*. May you have a pleasant journey to São Paulo. I hope you find a receptive audience among the Brazilians.'

'I will, don't you worry.' He placed his hat on his head and gave a knowing wink. 'I'm certain I will.'

Voegler tipped his hat, climbed into the car and departed.

Bruno got into a taxi himself and crossed the city with his face glued to the window, the expression on it somewhere between attentive and awe-struck. He asked the driver if they would pass Botafogo, since he wanted to see the Sugar Loaf up close. The Brazilian driver, chosen by the Condor Syndicate for his supposed ability to speak German, communicated rather fantastically with a peculiar Brazilian accent, which Bruno found highly entertaining. As they drove through Botafogo he pointed out Sugar Loaf and the Urca Casino, before setting off for Copacabana along the edge of the beach.

Bruno felt the heat, saw the bathers and people on the street, and thought to take off his suit jacket, roll up his shirtsleeves to the elbows and loosen the knot of the tie around his neck. The taxi pulled up in front of his hotel and, before he got out, he asked the taxi driver:

'How would you pronounce this name in Portuguese?'

He showed him Jonas Shmuel Kurtzberg's photoless passport.

'Jonas... ah... Ximael... Cruz... bergue...? Ah, sir, what a complicated name. Just say Jonas Samuel Cruz, it's much easier like that.'

'Thank you.'

He put the passport away and got out of the taxi. He checked into the hotel while his bags were taken to his room, then went up himself. He gave the bellboy a generous tip, shut the door and admired the spacious room that was all his.

The first thing he did was open the suitcase containing Jonas Kurtzberg's photographic equipment and examine the state of the camera and the lenses; a good Leica like that one did not come cheap. He closed the case.

He opened the other case he had brought with him, took out some papers and documents, and began to go through them one by one. Then he got undressed and took a cold shower. After all those days on board the Zeppelin he needed a proper wash.

On the bed, the suitcase with his clothes lay open. It had spent the journey in the ship's baggage compartment. He was in the act of choosing a clean outfit when the telephone in the room rang. He answered. The operator gave him a message. He wrote down an address.

Soon after, he went down to reception and ordered a taxi. No longer wearing that dark black suit and dressed instead in light grey trousers and jacket over a white linen shirt, his hair still wet from the shower, he looked like a different person, more relaxed and at ease. It is incredible how a new outfit and a different posture can transform one person into another.

When he entered the taxi, he said:

'Take me to Hotel Glória.'

It wasn't far. The taxi turned a few corners and stopped in front of the imposing neoclassical entrance to the grand white building—a hotel which, in those days, was only rivalled in luxury by the Copacabana Palace.

The reception was quite busy and he walked through it without anyone stopping him. He went straight to the lift and asked the attendant for the sixth floor, where the room whose number he had noted down awaited him.

He knocked at the door. A familiar voice answered in English.

'One moment, I'm coming.'

The door opened. William Hay did not look surprised to see him.

Bruno smiled.

'Thought you'd get away from me?'

Ten

BERLIN, May 1933.

The gramophone horn vibrates as it plays some piano music, and the projector flickers in the dark, smoke-filled room, casting its light and shadow on the wall: the film being shown is *Anders als die Andern* (Different from the Others).

On the screen, the violinist Paul Körner reads several newspaper stories about suicide cases— all deemed inexplicable, but which he knows are due to the blackmail of homosexual men, threatened with public exposure. Played by a young Conrad Veidt, before he achieved stardom in *Dr Caligari's Cabinet* and became the great leading man of German cinema, Körner comes across as an elegant, effeminate and sensitive homosexual. Körner watches a procession made up of Oscar Wilde, Tchaikovsky, Leonardo da Vinci and Frederick II of

Prussia, among many others, with successive swords of Damocles falling on them. An intertitle appears: *'None of the thousands who celebrated the brilliant artist suspected that he suffered from inclinations punished by society with banishment.'*

Then the young student Kurt appears, tormented by his parents, who wish him to get married, and by his friends, who want him to join their revels. But when he is surrounded by dancers and prostitutes, he rejects their advances. The madam looks suspiciously at the screen: *'If that boy's completely normal, then I'm a virgin.'*

Meanwhile, the violinist seeks help. First, with a hypnotist, unsuccessfully. Then he finds a doctor, one Magnus Hirschfeld, who appears on screen playing himself and says, to both the character and the audience: *'Love for one's own sex can be just as pure and noble as that for the opposite sex. This orientation is to be found among many respectable people in all levels of society.'*

Freed from his anguish, the violinist Körner starts to live his life. One of his first conquests is the hoodlum Bollek, whom he meets at a dance. But then, at a concert, Körner is approached by the young student Kurt, a great admirer who wishes to become his pupil.

'My deepest wish would come true if you were willing to be my teacher.'

Körner accepts. Nothing on-screen makes the film worthy of censorship, but for the attentive viewer, it's all there: teacher and student exchange intense looks and smiles, their embraces and handshakes always seem to last a second too long, the two men walk arm-in-arm though the park. And it's during one of these outings that they cross paths again with the no-good Bollek, who sees them both as an opportunity.

Blackmail follows: money or scandal. Körner is pushed to his limit, at which point he decides to prosecute Bollek for extortion. The blackmailer is found guilty and sent to prison; however, owing to paragraph 175 of the German Criminal Code, which condemns relationships between men, the victim is also found guilty. Public scandal follows and infamy befalls the great artist. Tormented, Körner overdoses on pills and commits suicide. During the funeral, a despairing young Kurt throws himself onto the coffin and says he will kill himself too. The whole scene is rather melodramatic. Then Dr Magnus Hirschfeld makes a reappearance, consoling the desperate lover: '*If you want to honour the memory of your friend, then you mustn't take your own life, but instead keep on living to change the prejudices whose victim—one of countless many—this dead man has become. This is the life task I assign to you. Just as Zola struggled on behalf of one man who languished innocently in prison, what matters now is to restore honour and justice to the many thousands before us, with us and after us. Through knowledge to justice!'* The film draws to a close.

The lights are turned on in J. Kurtzberg's studio, Moderne Fotokunst, a large penthouse apartment in a modern apartment block. The space is lit by a long skylight, which can be covered and uncovered according to the light desired. One of the doors leads to a room that has been transformed into a darkroom for developing photos, the other to the bathroom. A partition hides a double bed and one of Joseph Pohl's simple and practical 'bachelor's wardrobes'. There are glass-topped tables, metallic cupboards, an ice box and half a dozen Brno chairs, Jonas's latest Bauhausian obsession which, together with two Barcelona armchairs and a metal tubular sofa with leather cushions and a few drapes, provided the seating in that makeshift clandestine cinema.

Someone begins opening bottles of beer and pouring them into glasses. The English boy gets up from the armchair, takes a glass and walks over to Jonas.

'I must say, I wasted no time getting used to the talkies,' Willy Hay comments. 'Now, whenever I see a silent film, the music doesn't quite seem to fit. There's no harmony between sound and image at all—you'll see characters going through all sorts of suffering on screen to the sound of a foxtrot.'

'You're a harsh critic,' Jonas replies. 'Is that all you can come up with? Picking apart the technical aspects of the film?'

Willy takes a sip of his beer and smiles his cunning smile.

'Oh, I'm only teasing, you silly ass. To be honest, I did find it a little too didactic and lacking in artistry, but it's refreshing to see someone like us on the screen, plain as day. I'm trying to imagine how the film must have been received when it was released… How long ago was it? Fourteen years?'

Yes, Jonas confirms. The film had been very important to him at the time. He was sixteen when the world emerged from the self-destructive nightmare of the war that was meant to end all wars. A year later, he watched *Anders als die Andern* at a packed screening. Despite the debate surrounding the film, the topic was a novelty, its melodramatic plot entertaining. That same year, a group of doctors, intellectuals and politicians had gathered in a mansion near Berlin's Tiergarten, where they had established the world's first independent institution dedicated to the study of sexuality and a cure for suffering related to it. Its founder, Magnus Hirschfeld, had dedicated his life to dispelling preconceptions created by religious morality and demonstrating through science that so-called sexual anomalies were not pathologies, but rather biological characteristics, as natural as skin colour or colour blindness. With its motto of 'through science, justice', its aim was to repeal the notorious paragraph 175 of the German Penal Code, which criminalized men who had intimate relationships with other men.

Jonas followed all the news about the film in the papers: nationalist groups and antisemites interrupted screenings, alleging that they were 'poisoning morality'; a pastor accused the film of wanting to turn the young into homosexuals by portraying such people as being equal to 'normal and healthy' members of society, citing the story they had 'heard on good authority' of a homosexual who went through the streets luring children to follow him, like the Pied Piper of Hamelin. With the patience of a saint, Dr Hirschfeld tried to explain that no one, not even a film, can change a person's sexual orientation.

At the same time, Jonas was beginning to explore the possibilities of photography, composing images with light and shade, but felt that his work—photos of friends and landscapes—was excessively formal and somewhat sterile. He realized that he had not only the right but also the obligation to put more of himself into what he did, to liberate himself through his gaze which, lacking fear or uncertainty, would acquire the honesty that would make his work more personal. Those were the best years of Bauhaus and the surrealists, from Chirico's paintings to Man Ray's photographs; Jonas absorbed it all, combining it with his era's fascination with the athletic body, physical health and the hikes in the great outdoors popular with youth movements.

But men like Dr Hirschfeld, who sought to educate and enlighten through science, and Adolf Brand, with his impracticable egoist anarchism and the elitism of his journal *Der Eigene*, aiming to forge a path towards intellectual prestige, belonged to an older generation. They were creatures of the nineteenth century. It was only a matter of time before Jonas became associated with the editor Radszuweit.

Friedrich Radszuweit and his League for Human Rights belonged to a more modern branch of the movement, born in the twentieth century. And if Radszuweit believed in anything, it was that fulfilling a need for *entertainment* was as essential, liberating and important as educating their audience. How else, he said, would they reach a less enlightened audience, for whom Hirschfeld's scientific treatises or Brand's ambitious literary journal were inaccessible?

'It's not a *great* film,' Jonas concluded. 'But it was good entertainment at the time, and it helped me see many things more clearly.'

The two drank their beers in silence for a while. The mood in the studio was oppressive, filled with a tension not even the alcohol could dissipate. The sword of Damocles had returned to hang over everyone's head in recent months, ever since the Nazi Party had won a majority in the Reichstag, guaranteeing, with their customary sarcasm and cynicism, that they would 'respect the constitution'.

'I'm considering going back to England,' Willy said. 'You should come with me. You heard what happened this week at Dr Hirschfeld's institute, didn't you?'

Jonas nodded. It was just the latest in a spate of attacks their community had suffered ever since Hitler became chancellor. His editor, Radszuweit, had died the year before, believing that the attacks being made in Nazi publications against homosexuals would fizzle out without coming to very much, but by the beginning of that year all the bars and dance halls for homosexuals had been closed, even the legendary El Dorado. Just last Saturday, the Institut für Sexualwissenschaft had been broken into and trashed by members of the Hitler Youth who had shouted 'Burn Hirschfeld!' as they beat up the staff and took away the contents of the library for a public book burning. Dr Hirschfeld himself had been abroad, travelling to promote his most recent book. He never returned to Germany.

'Things are getting very strange, very quickly,' Willy said.

'Things won't stay like this for long,' Jonas assured him. 'The other parties, the political system, they'll all have a moderating effect on them. And this anti-Jewish thing is just propaganda. You'll see, they'll have better things to do than to keep bothering Jews. Besides, where would I go? I was born here, this is my country. The Nazis are just a bunch of fanatics, they don't understand my position.'

'What position, Jonas? You're a Jew. A *Mischling*, as they say. Didn't you see Goebbels talking the other day? I did, and it was horrifying. The way he speaks, the hysterical tone, the religious language, as if Hitler were a new messiah. He seems maddened with hatred for your people.'

'What nonsense. My mother was German. I don't care one bit about religion, as you well know. Nor did my father. We've been in this country for centuries. The Jews the Nazis are raging about are simply the immigrants who came from Eastern Europe after the war. They heaped the blame onto them for everything that went wrong and... What is it, Willy?'

Willy seemed distracted, looking around him at the other men in the room. He cut Jonas off with a raised hand.

'Can you hear that?'

What had begun as a murmur of voices soon swelled into an angry roar, surging up through the corridors of the building towards them before bursting into the studio: eight or nine men in brown shirts with swastika armbands, chanting their slogan: '*Deutschland über alles.*'

Unbeknown to those present at the film screening, when Hirschfeld's institute had been broken into earlier that week, the Nazis had seized not only the library but also a list of the names and addresses of all those who had ever been associated with the institute. And Jonas Kurtzberg's name had been on the list.

In fact, that night the Nazi militias were combing libraries and bookshops all over the city, confiscating books by authors deemed socialists, pacifists, Jews, homosexuals or in some way hostile to the Nazis. There was a bookshop on the ground floor of Jonas's building, next to a sign advertising 'J. Kurtzberg, *Moderne Fotokunst*' and directing visitors to the top floor. One of the Brownshirts who came marching into the studio that evening was Heinrich Wagner, a young Bavarian with pale blond hair whom Jonas had danced with at one of the extravagant *Puppenbälle* before Heinrich posed for a few photos that were never published. Jonas never did find out whether that was pure coincidence or whether Heinrich had convinced the group to climb the stairs.

The Brownshirts' eruption into the studio sparked uproar. Martin König, who had worked as a bouncer at El Dorado until it was closed and who had been harbouring a murderous rage against the Nazis ever since, threw himself at the militiamen, lashing out, bursting open one of their noses and smashing a beer bottle in another's face. Rudolf Richter, a journalist and former lover of Jonas, grabbed one of the studio's Brno chairs and broke it over the head of another Nazi, before rushing out of the studio, pushing his way through the melee; when a Brownshirt grabbed hold of him as he went through the door, the two men tumbled down the stairs together.

Jonas grabbed a handful of Willy Hay's shirt, pulling him over to the window and out onto the fire escape. They ran down it like a pair of lunatics, not looking back, hearing only the echoes of shouts, glass breaking and chairs being smashed.

At the bottom, they emerged into a dark dead-end side alley between the buildings, poorly lit by the light from a street lamp spilling in from the pavement. But two shadows blocked the light and their path to safety. Before they could react, Jonas was bent double by a punch in the gut from the first shape; Willy recoiled against the wall, cornered by the second, and began to speak very quickly in English, pleading with his attacker not to hurt him. The man put him in an armlock and grabbed him by the hair, twisting his face towards Jonas.

Jonas was hit with a piece of pipe and fell, curling into a ball in an attempt to protect his head from more blows. Then the kicks began. Jonas vomited. The man crouched down and punched him in the head, then took him by the hair and rubbed Jonas's face in his own vomit, as he shouted: 'You depraved degenerate, I'm doing your family a favour!'

Jonas raised his head, but his face was so swollen and running with blood that he could hardly see. All he could make out of his attacker was a pair of jackboots, which walked a few paces away from him down the alley, before a voice said:

'Come here.'

He heard the click of a hammer being cocked.

'Come here or die.'

Jonas dragged himself along the ground, trying not to put any weight on his arm, which seemed to be broken. When he reached the jackboots, he heard the voice say:

'Lick.'

He looked up in confusion, and with his one eye that was not swollen shut, he saw the man who was ready to kill him, and whose face was now visible in the light of the street lamp.

Build: medium. Face shape: oval. Eye colour: grey. Accent: Munich. To the end of his days, Jonas would never forget that face, which just months later he discovered belonged to a man called Otto Klein.

'Lick or die.'

Jonas obeyed. He opened his aching mouth, slowly stuck out his tongue, and licked the tip of the boot, leaving a trail of saliva and blood on it.

'Get this into your skull, queer: you're nothing now, and I am everything.'

He gave Jonas a final kick in the face and left. Before he passed out, Jonas's last memory from that night was the sickly-sweet taste of blood filling his mouth, the two Brownshirts walking out of the alley, their dark outlines silhouetted against the light, and Willy crouching by his side, babbling unintelligibly through a fit of tears.

He woke up in a hospital room with his arm in a sling, barely able to feel his face, numbed as it was with painkillers and morphine. Even so, the doctor said he'd been lucky: despite the damage to his ribs, and once the swelling from the bruises had gone down, the forty or so stitches to his face, arms and thorax had been removed, and the broken arm had spent two months in plaster,

Jonas would be left with only a few scars. It was a miracle that he had survived.

His brother and sister-in-law came to visit him once the dressings had come off. His sister-in-law began to cry the moment she saw him; his brother gasped. Jonas, who still had not seen the condition his face was in, asked for a mirror, and his sister-in-law found one in her bag. When he saw his swollen face, covered in bruises and looking like it had been sewn up by Kandinsky, he quipped that now he could finally attempt a career in cinema.

'I'm going to be the new Boris Karloff.'

Then he had a fit of giggles, rapidly followed by a fit of tears.

Willy also came to visit him. He told Jonas he had returned to the studio the next day and had managed to save quite a lot of the negatives, some of his equipment and a few photos and magazines, but had heard nothing more from their friends.

What Willy had witnessed on Opernplatz that same day was something he could never have imagined. He watched as they burned on a huge bonfire Hemingway and Wells and Huxley and Joyce and Fitzgerald and Kafka and Tolstoy and Gorky and Dostoyevsky and Musil and Gide and Brecht and Einstein and Zweig and Schnitzler and Nabokov and Proust and Zola;

Hellen Keller and Walter Benjamin and Lukács and Marcuse, Oscar Wilde and Radclyffe Hall and Isaac Babel and Herman Hesse and Jack London and Joseph Conrad and Mark Twain and Thomas Mann and Victor Hugo and John dos Passos and Erich Maria Remarque, even Bambi by Felix Salten, all of them burned in the fire; he watched Gropius and Kandinsky's Bauhaus and Freud's psychoanalysis burn; they burned books by foreigners and emigrants, books by the excessively intellectual and by democratic liberals, and most of all they burned books by everyone who had ever expressed, orally or on the page, any criticisms of the Nazis or their leader.

Jonas discovered that Adolf Brand, editor of *Der Eigene*, had sent a letter to all his collaborators announcing the end of the homosexual movement in Germany. One of its main leaders, Kurt Hiller, had been imprisoned by the Gestapo and sent to the Oranienburg prison camp. Others simply began to disappear. Lotte Hahm had been attacked at the Violetta club, and Jonas had heard that many lesbians were hurrying to marry their male homosexual friends, to avoid further persecution. The Nazis spoke of a new empire, a Third Reich, against which the third sex would stand no chance. This time, when Willy once more raised the idea of leaving, Jonas accepted. Let's get out of Germany, away from Europe.

Let's go somewhere sunny where the music warms you and the drink refreshes you.

'Let's go to Brazil. You'll like it there,' Willy said.

September 1933.

At the train station, Jonas Kurtzberg says goodbye to his brother, sister-in-law and nephew, little Josef, a ten-year-old with a keen eye and a vivid imagination who has been like a son to him.

The boy hands his uncle a farewell card inside an envelope. On it, Josef has drawn his uncle wearing a hat and raising a hand to say goodbye, inside an airship that is smiling like a friendly flying whale. Jonas puts the envelope containing the drawing in his coat pocket and smiles, ruffling the boy's hair. Then he kisses his sister-in-law, before hugging his brother tightly and telling him that, sooner or later, they will meet again. It is the last time he will see them alive. Despite the innumerable attempts he makes to get them out of Germany, in five years' time the three of them will be taken to the Sachsenhausen camp. He never hears from them again.

Jonas is travelling alone. The nine hours it takes to reach Friedrichshafen pass slowly. He finds himself constantly touching his coat pocket, anxiously making sure his passport is still there. In a matter of hours, his life will be in the hands of a balloon, and he will be out of reach of the government and its militias.

Those months of recuperation after the attack were tortuous: going out onto the street triggered panic attacks; a potential threat hid round every corner; nobody was the same any more—from the kind lady taking her pooch for a walk to the baker from whom he had always bought his bread. Any one of them might have voted for *him*, might sympathize with his hysterical and violent ideas, might smile and wish him good morning while secretly wishing for him to be wiped off the face of the earth. Everything was black and white now, the very streets became mazes formed of buildings that were merely geometrical shapes projecting elongated shadows, inhabited by vampires and *golems* waiting for the moment when Jonas would be led like a sleepwalker to the office where they would decide his ultimate destiny. It was then he decided that, if anything went wrong before his departure date, he would end his life on his own terms. He obtained a cyanide capsule from a pharmacist, and for six long months he walked around with it in his coat pocket, touching it every time he felt anxious or cornered, to check it was still there, like a protective amulet.

Because what he had heard from those who had been imprisoned and managed to get out had shaken him deeply. A few days before leaving, he had met Rudolf

Richter, the ex-boyfriend who had escaped the studio and tumbled down the stairs with the Brownshirt. He had nonetheless been imprisoned and sent to the Columbia-Haus camp. Family connections had got him out, but he was now a complete wreck.

'They're reforming the prisons,' Rudolf told him. 'They say they're going to be converted into a new kind of prison camp.'

Rudolf told him about the back-breaking jobs homosexual prisoners such as himself were made to do, far more punishing than the work given to other prisoners, since it was widely believed hard work would cure them. He talked about the rapes he and other homosexuals suffered, the beatings, how their testicles were dipped into boiling water, their nails torn out, the things the guards would shove up their arses for their own amusement, some so long that they perforated their intestines, causing them to bleed to death, and how some were simply beaten to death. In short, how they were treated as the lowest of the low. Because in the eyes of the Nazis, who worshipped their own masculinity above all else, they were even lower than Gypsies or Jews.

Rudolf had managed to get out, but his name was still on a list. They kept lots of names on lots of lists. At the beginning of the year, when the Reichstag had approved the law that gave Hitler sweeping powers, the first thing the Nazis had done was to persecute professors, doctors and lawyers who weren't aligned with the government. Not long before Jonas left, a new law was passed allowing the Nazis to strip citizenship from anyone considered 'undesirable'. He was certain his name was already on some list. Except his name was no longer Jonas Kurtzberg.

Rudolf Richter ended up being imprisoned again, together with Martin König, the enormous bouncer who had knocked down a bunch of Brownshirts when they invaded Jonas's studio. This time, they were sent to the Buchenwald camp, where it was customary to give homosexual prisoners the task of preparing clay moulds for the guards' target practice. But when the guards saw the prisoners wearing the armbands with pink triangles, they chose to aim directly at them. Heinrich Wagner, the beautiful, young, blond Bavarian who had led the militiamen to Jonas's studio, didn't fare much better. A year after the studio invasion, he was in the Hanselbauer Hotel in Munich, in bed with and in the arms of *Stabschef* Edmund Heines, who was very close to Ernst Röhm, when Hitler and Himmler decided to eliminate the entire leadership of the SA. It was the Night of the Long Knives, and young Heinrich was executed that same morning, not before receiving the dubious honour of being attacked by the Führer himself, who had slapped him out of irritation—at least, that's what the official version said. That Röhm, Heines and many high-ranking SA officers were homosexuals was an open secret, but it provided the perfect justification for an 'internal clean-up' that was, at the end of the day, simply a power struggle.

When he arrives at the Luftschiffbau Zeppelin airfield, Jonas hands over his ticket and has his passport checked. Everything is in order; everyone who needed to be bribed has been bribed. All his money, title deeds and shares have been used to falsify his documents and turn him into the police detective Bruno Brückner, a deliberate choice made under the assumption—one which proved correct—that, in a society based on obedience to power, the legitimacy of authority figures would not be questioned. When he disembarks in Brazil, safe and sound, he will be Jonas Kurtzberg again, and for this purpose he keeps, in the false bottom of the briefcase he uses to carry his photographic equipment, an envelope containing his original passport, the photograph carefully peeled off with the help of a steaming kettle.

Another deliberate choice was to fly in an airship, something he had always wanted to do. Three or four days in the air would be far better than a fortnight rolling about on the high seas. There was something extravagant about the idea, a final, elegant turn with which to draw his old life to a close.

He watches Willy board too, and the two act like complete strangers, an extra act of caution for someone already drowning in worries, forever nervously touching the cyanide capsule in his coat pocket to check it's still there.

When the LZ 127 *Graf Zeppelin* takes flight, Bruno breathes a sigh of relief, watching Germany fade away through the window. There's nothing left for him in that country. Even if he weren't Jewish, even if he weren't homosexual, anyone considered too artistic or intellectual is in danger. Bertolt Brecht was the first to leave, for Denmark. Fritz Lang, invited by Goebbels to be in charge of the UFA studios, said thank you, I'll think about it, then fled for Paris. Kandinsky followed him, while Paul Klee emigrated to Switzerland, where Thomas Mann had already gone, having been warned by his children that it might no longer be safe to return to Germany. And Conrad Veidt, married to a Jewish woman, escaped with her to London.

But many would stay. The ones who were neither socialists, nor communists, nor pacifists, nor Jews, nor homosexuals, who were not overly interested in foreign culture, who did not create art that was too modern, who were fine with not saying anything that went against the leader's will, since the leader was always right. These people would accept what Klaus Mann later called a pact with Mephistopheles.

On the 16th of October 1933, while he was waiting in the hotel in Recife, he saw that face again. What was that man from the other side of the ocean doing there? He didn't know, he didn't want to know, nor did it matter. If he'd had a gun in his hands, he could have killed him right there in the hotel restaurant, in front of everyone.

On the taxi journey back to Campo de Jiquiá, he hatched his plan. And as soon as he entered the cabin and checked the new passenger list that was delivered before departure, he saw that it contained one new German name: Otto Klein. He took the cyanide capsule from his pocket. It was the size of a rifle bullet, as thick as his little finger, and it occurred to him that it would be very easy to remove it from his pocket, keep it hidden in his hand and sprinkle the contents onto a plate of food or into a drink. He drank his whisky and soda and went to Willy's cabin to sketch out his plan.

'He's not getting out of here alive.'

'You don't want him dropping dead at the dinner table,' Willy said.

'I'll split the dose in half, it won't be immediate.'

'And how will you give it to him?'

'At dinner. Or breakfast. Or lunch, or at the next dinner—there won't be any shortage of opportunities. I'll improvise.'

'He'll recognize you.'

'He won't.'

'How can you be so certain?'

'I just *know* he won't.'

It wasn't only because he had been attacked down a dark and poorly lit alley, or because Bruno couldn't have been the only person beaten up by Otto Klein during those months, or because he who hits soon forgets, but he who is hit never does. The reality is that, while some people look far younger than their age at thirty, some look far older. And every time he had looked in the mirror since getting out of hospital, Jonas realized he had moved from the former category to the latter, ageing ten years in five months.

It is said that luck is nothing more than a name for when preparation meets opportunity. Otto Klein happened to sit next to him at the table. As predicted, he did not recognize him. It wasn't just Jonas's posture—it was his easy, calm bearing, one of cold, vengeful tranquillity. The costume helped too: the final touch, the Nazi party pin, jarred so strongly with his true image that even someone who knew him well would look again before being sure it was really him, Jonas Kurtzberg, wearing that badge.

The cyanide capsule was in his pocket. All that was needed was an exchange of glances between him and Willy for the message to be received. With his devilish, public-schoolboy charm, Willy let his spoon fall gently onto the carpeted floor and took the baroness's one for himself. She only noticed the piece of cutlery was missing when dessert was served.

'Oh, I think you have taken my dessert spoon, Mr Hay.'

'No, this one's mine,' the Englishman said. 'Perhaps it fell under the table? Let me see... oh yes. There it is, by Herr Klein's feet.'

That was the cue for Jonas to unscrew the capsule. The moment they all looked under the table was the moment he, holding the capsule between his fingers, poured the cyanide over Otto Klein's ice cream.

Klein ate, and Willy set about annoying him in the most clinical way possible. Klein went to bed. It was now only a matter of time.

At dawn, Jonas, having woken up bright and early and seen that the lavatory door was locked, peeked into Otto Klein's cabin to check that he was the one locked inside the WC. Then he had an idea. He went back to his cabin and found the photos and magazines he had brought with him, in the false back of his suitcase. He separated the photograph of Fridolin from all the other boys he had shot, along with two magazines, and placed them in the briefcase carrying his camera, lenses and some photographic material, including the vial of Prussian blue. He also found his original passport, without the photo. He threw it all into Otto Klein's cabin, the passport casually tossed onto the floor, next to the sofa bed.

One last detail: seeing Otto Klein's suit hanging from the coat rack, he searched the pockets and found his passport. He took a pen and made a few small marks on the visa stamps. He went through Otto Klein's suitcase, his real suitcase, and took it to his cabin. Then he waited.

Commander Eckener asking him to lead the investigation was a rather agreeable bonus. In a position of authority, he was able to pronounce on which passport was real and which a forgery, to interrogate suspects and draw attention to their suspicious features: the baroness's obsession with Lucrezia Borgia, the hydrochloric acid in the doctor's suitcase, even Willy's good manners, which made him resemble one of those gentleman spies from John Buchan's books, lending plausibility to the idea that the victim was a communist agent in disguise. And, last of all, a personal touch: making the Nazis dispose of the body of one of their own, burying the truth at the bottom of Guanabara Bay.

'Thought you'd get away from me?' Jonas Kurtzberg said the moment Willy opened the door of his room at Hotel Glória.

'Not for a second.'

As soon as the door was closed, they kissed. Removing their shoes, tearing off jackets and belts and undoing the buttons of each other's shirts and flies, they fell onto the bed and made love for the first time in months, with an aggressive, furious satisfaction, before collapsing in exhaustion and ecstasy, their sweat-drenched skin sticking to the sheets.

They laughed as they remembered those last few days: that horrific line-up and their speechifying on 'degenerate art', the expression on Willy's face upon being surprised by the interrogation and having to improvise, one minute throwing Fridolin's reputation to the lions, the next suggesting a communist plot. Ah, if only Willy had seen the baroness's face when she talked about her nephew Fridolin, 'such an angel, he goes to mass every day'. And that odious doctor, Willy recalled, incapable of spotting a Jew sitting right in front of him while practically decreeing that Otto Klein was a direct descendant of King David. They chuckled.

Jonas reached for his jacket.

'Oh, damn. I left my cigarettes in the other hotel room.'

'Let's go out and buy some,' Willy suggested. 'We'll take a stroll along the promenade, watch the world go by.'

They dressed and took the lift down.

On their way, they stopped at a magazine stand and saw the advert: 'Veado Brand cigarettes: for posh and poor alike'. Jonas bought a packet, took out one cigarette for himself and another for Willy, who lit them with his lighter, closed the lid in a quick flourish and returned it to his pocket.

The sky twinkled with aquamarine blue over the sandy beach, which rang with the cries and laughter of boys at play; ladies in black bathing suits and straw hats sitting beneath sunshades waved at the children not to go out too deep in the water; men and boys wore ridiculously long bathing suits, with waistlines at belly button height. On the promenade, ice-cold coconuts glimmered and butter was melted over cobs of corn in their vendors' hands, while a fresh breeze blew, carrying with it the salty scent of the sea air, the smell of the horizon. It was all wide open, all sheer possibility.

The two of them walked for some time, following the wavy black and white tiles of the beach promenade, before Willy said:

'What I don't understand is why he was in Recife.'

'Who, Otto Klein? It was just a coincidence,' Jonas said.

Jonas had also wondered about that. Until that trip, he had never learnt his attacker's identity. He had searched Klein's case for clues, found commercial letters, stamped documents, the *Small Trader's Pocket Directory*, and had discovered that he was indeed nothing more than a merchant who, until that year, had simply been the owner of a small Munich emporium, an example of the petty bourgeoisie that was the Nazis' political support base. Some letters in Otto Klein's case showed that he, like many other Germans, sponsored and organized one of the shooting clubs which served as training grounds for pro-Nazi militias. The kind of militias that, during the election, used to go out onto the streets to confront the communists or anyone who dared to wear red.

But now Hitler was chancellor. And Otto Klein had left behind the resentful mediocrity of his life as a small-time trader in Munich and begun to get generous supply contracts and good contacts in Brazil for coffee importation. Still, none of this answered the question: who, really, was Otto Klein?

He was nobody. Or rather, he was everybody that is nobody. He was all of those who felt humiliated by the war's great collective defeat and the harsh reparations imposed on Germany. All those who had nothing to define them except the sum of their petty failures and personal frustrations and who, incapable of confronting them, had instead fallen prey to an all-encompassing sense of paranoia, messianic mysticism and a hatred of everything that was different from them: the universal cause of all ills, the *other*, the great trickster at the heart of the worldwide conspiracy that was the explanation for all problems, both real and imaginary. He was everyone trapped by the economic crisis, stewing in social resentment and tormented by puritanical moralism, nourished by more than a century of nationalist tirades assuring them of their own superiority. Everyone whose misconceptions and ignorance and fantasies of power were channelled into speeches offering simplistic and deranged solutions by orators so grotesque no one took them seriously until it was too late.

Ultimately, Otto Klein was all of those who clung to whoever supplied them with a new sense of belonging, of identity, an identity brought together by an unconditional devotion to a leader who had turned the sum of their failures into an emblem of pride, in a community where the concept of 'fanaticism' was now seen as a positive quality, a synonym for heroism and virtue. Now they would know who they were. They would no longer be alone, for now they would be part of something bigger, a cause that would become so noble that no scruple could get in its way: the expurgation and purification of everything that wasn't a reflection of themselves, and which, therefore, would weaken their nation: Jews, Gypsies, Slavs, homosexuals and 'degenerates' in general; the old, the weak, the mentally ill and all psychiatric patients; and also communists, socialists, anarchists, pacifists and indeed every ideology except their own, which would then become no longer an ideology but rather the only possible truth, the only possible identity, amalgamated with national identity until it was impossible to separate the German from the Nazi, and everything that wasn't one would not be the other. Otto Klein was nobody and he was many.

'And still, they're nothing more than gangsters,' Jonas finished. 'Neighbourhood ruffians, jackbooted thugs and backstreet toughs, now elevated to the highest posts. I see no difference between them and the mafiosos from American films.'

'Easy, old chap, that's all behind us,' Willy said. 'Europe is behind us, we're in Brazil now. Let's have some fun for a few days, make the most of the time we have, because I fear Daddy will want me back in London before long.'

'I need work. I need money. I need to try to get my brother's family out,' Jonas said.

'I'll make some calls, talk to some of Daddy's acquaintances, see what we can do for you,' Willy assured him. 'And there must be a well-organized Jewish community here. It won't be difficult for someone with your talent for photography, with your eye, to find work. Forget about all that now, forget about Otto Klein. You don't need to pass as someone else any more. You can go back to being good old Jonas Shmuel Kurtzberg… Or Jonas Samuel Cruz.'

A bronzed, athletic youth wearing only a short bathing costume, his body a sculpture of muscles and tendons, his skin speckled with droplets like water on rubber, walked past them, coming from the beach. They turned their heads at the same time, and the boy, noticing that he was being observed by both gringos, stopped and repaid their gazes with a luminous, wicked smile, ambiguously suggestive.

Yes, Jonas thought, as he felt the heat of the summer sun on his face. He could foresee the shadows in his path. There would be despair, deep sadness and a feeling of impotence in the face of the machinery of the world. But, at least for now, at least for a moment, he needed to feel the summer sun against his face, the salt sea on his skin, and live each extra moment of existence he had won as intensely as possible. That other feeling, which would later be called 'survivor's guilt', that lump in the throat every time he remembered the family and friends he had lost, meant that Jonas was for a long time unable to identify this as happiness. But, at least for now, it was a feeling of contentment, a furious satisfaction at having thwarted all those who wanted him to be erased, at having dared to stay alive. For if there was something he would never in his life feel guilty about, it was having made Otto Klein finally become a good Nazi, in the only conceivable way a Nazi can be good: by being dead.

Postal stamp Z-9, from 1930, issued by Correios do Brasil to be used exclusively on correspondence sent via Zeppelin airmail.

Author's Note

I am grateful for the readings, comments and encouragement of Carlos André Moreira, Matheus Gonçalves, Marcelo Ferroni, Marianna Teixeira Soares, Rafael Bassi, Rafael Kasper, Raquel Cozer, Tamara Machado Pias and Tobias Carvalho; to my editor André Conti and his polymath's eye; and to Professor Ricardo Timm de Souza, whose classes on the language of idolatrous thought and philatelic fascination with the Zeppelin lit the spark that would result in this book.